GROUNDED

GROUNDED

Kate Klise

Feiwel and Friends · New York

LEMONT PUBLIC LIBRARY DISTRICT
50 East Wend Street
Lemont, IL 60439-6439

Although inspired by real people and places, the characters
and events portrayed in this book are entirely fictional.

A FEIWEL AND FRIENDS BOOK
An Imprint of Macmillan

GROUNDED. Copyright © 2010 by Kate Klise. All rights reserved.
Distributed in Canada by H.B. Fenn and Company Ltd.
Printed in October 2010 in the United States of America
by R. R. Donnelley & Sons Company, Harrisonburg, Virginia.
For information, address
Feiwel and Friends, 175 Fifth Avenue, New York, N.Y. 10010.

Library of Congress Cataloging-in-Publication Data
Klise, Kate.
Grounded / Kate Klise. — 1st ed.
      p.   cm.
Summary: After her father, brother, and sister are killed in a plane crash, twelve-year-old
Daralynn's life in tiny Digginsville, Missouri, continues as her mother turns angry and
embittered, her grandmother becomes senile, and her flamboyant aunt continues to run the
Summer Sunset Retirement Home for Distinguished Gentlemen, while being courted by
the owner of the town's new crematorium.
ISBN: 978-0-312-57039-2
[1. Grief—Fiction.   2. Swindlers and swindling—Fiction.
3. Missouri—History—20th century—Fiction.]   I. Title.
PZ7.K684Gr 2010   [Fic]—dc22   2010013008

Book design by Véronique Lefèvre Sweet

Feiwel and Friends logo designed by Filomena Tuosto

First Edition: 2010

1   3   5   7   9   10   8   6   4   2

www.feiwelandfriends.com

FREMONT PUBLIC LIBRARY DISTRICT

3 1559 00223 2278

Give sorrow words; the grief that does not speak
Whispers the o'er-fraught heart and bids it break.
—William Shakespeare, *Macbeth*

GROUNDED

ONE

Grounded in Digginsville

I'M ALIVE TODAY because I was grounded. Maybe that sounds odd to you, but it's true.

I was grounded by Mother for going fishing at Doc Lake without her permission. That's the only reason I wasn't in Daddy's plane when it crashed and killed him, my brother, and my little sister.

I was home sulking on the front porch, mad that I couldn't go flying with the others. Mother was inside, ironing in the kitchen and listening to "Swap Line." That was the name of a radio program. For five minutes every hour on the hour, folks would call in to the radio station and try to swap something they had for something somebody else had.

My mother loved "Swap Line." Nothing entertained her more than hearing people describe the junk they had in their basements and attics. For a woman who kept her house neat as a pin, listening to "Swap Line" was like listening to people confess their sins. Mother kept the kitchen radio turned on all day long so she wouldn't miss it.

Even from the front porch, I could hear her through the screen door, talking to the radio while she ironed.

"Bud Mosley, you've been trying to swap that cracked aquarium for three *weeks*," Mother said, howling with delight.

My mother knew everyone who called in to "Swap Line." She even knew their junk. In bigger cities, folks had news to listen to every hour. We had "Swap Line."

"Daralynn!" she called to me from the kitchen. "Come and listen to 'Swap Line.' It's a good one."

"I don't want to listen!" I hollered from the porch.

Truth was, I *did* want to listen. I was as hooked on "Swap Line" as anyone. But I suppose on that Sunday afternoon in late October I wanted to pout more.

I was kicking leaves in the yard when the state trooper's car pulled up in front of our house. It was

Jimmy Chuck Walters. He's the one who told us about the engine failing on Daddy's plane.

He told us in the kitchen. When he finished, Mother didn't cry. She just closed the front door, turned off the iron, and called Mamaw, my grandmother, who lived next door.

Right away, they started planning the funeral: *One service or three? Granite gravestone or marble? A reception at church or at the house?*

I wasn't much help in making the funeral arrangements. My brain couldn't take in all the information. It was like an old tree you can't fully see by just standing in front of it. You have to step around it slowly to understand how big it really is.

The world had changed. That much I knew.

But I confess the first thing I thought after I heard about the crash was: *I'd swap Bud Mosley a cracked aquarium for this.*

My second thought was: *If I'm the only kid left in my family, I bet Mother won't ground me as much anymore. I bet I won't get grounded again for the rest of my life.*

TWO

Hello, Dolly

You wouldn't believe all the dolls I got after that.

For days, people drove up our driveway. Usually they'd leave their cars running while they knocked on the front door.

"I'm so sorry, honey." That's what most folks said when I opened the door. Then they'd hand me a doll.

Others whispered: "We're praying for you." And then they'd hand me a doll.

Cloth dolls. Plastic dolls. Creepy baby dolls with giant pink faces. Curvaceous Barbies. Barbie knock-offs. Beautiful Crissy dolls with glossy red hair just asking to be pulled.

I was buried alive in dolls.

And unlike the crockpots filled with ham and beans that arrived with the owners' names written on masking tape, the dolls weren't meant to be returned. They were for me. To keep.

One day Miss Avis Brown from *The Digginsville Daily Quill* came to the house. She wrote a story about me and all the dang dolls I was getting. It ran on the front page under the headline:

Hello, Dolly!
12-Year-Old Girl Receives 237 Dolls After Family Tragedy

That's when a lot of people in town started calling me Dolly instead of my real name, which is Daralynn Oakland.

What everyone forgot was that *I* wasn't the one who *liked* dolls. That was my little sister, Lilac Rose. She was Mother's favorite.

Lilac Rose was named after the flowers Daddy gave Mother on their first date. Just like her name, Lilac Rose was pretty and prickly, especially when Mother brushed her hair.

Even at the funeral home, Mother spent hours bossing Lilac Rose's golden hair into perfect banana curls as she lay stretched out in her casket.

Nearly every bone in Lilac Rose's body was broken, but she sure looked pretty. That was important to Mother.

Lilac Rose was nine years old when she died.

Wayne Junior was sixteen. He was Daddy's favorite. My brother wanted to be a pilot for Ozark Air Lines, just like Daddy. He probably could've done it, too. Wayne Junior was smart and good at math. But he wasn't as handsome as Daddy.

My daddy was the most handsome man in Digginsville. Every lady in town admired his blue eyes and sandy-blond hair. Even the girls in my class used to say he was more handsome than Paul Newman and Robert Redford combined, which filled me with pride and embarrassment, combined.

I didn't inherit good looks from my parents. With my brown ponytail and hazel eyes, I looked more like Daddy's sister, Aunt Josie, only without her makeup and dyed red hair.

It was a rare occasion to see Aunt Josie without her Passion Red lipstick and drawn-on eyebrows. In fact, the first time I ever saw Aunt Josie without her makeup was the day of the crash. She burst through our front door without even knocking.

"I just heard the news from Jimmy Chuck Walters!" Aunt Josie wailed. "It can't be true! Oh, Hattie, is it true?"

"It's true, all right," Mother said stonily.

That made Aunt Josie cry harder. "Those beautiful children," she moaned, collapsing in our front hallway. "Lilac Rose. Wayne Junior. And my sweet baby brother!"

Mother just stood there with her hands on her bony hips, staring straight ahead.

"How can it *be*?" Aunt Josie continued. "Oh my God in heaven above!"

Mother snapped. "Don't make a show of it, Josie," she directed. And then she walked upstairs and started picking out clothes for Lilac Rose, Wayne Junior, and Daddy to wear in their caskets.

I might not have been Mother's favorite, but I wasn't in last place. That distinction was held by Aunt Josie, who'd been at the bottom of Mother's list for as long as I could remember.

Aunt Josie's crying that day of the crash—the messiness of it all, the display of uncontrolled emotions, the fact that Aunt Josie wasn't even wearing lipstick—was contrary to everything my mother stood for. All she could do was wait for Aunt Josie to be on her way.

Looking back, I know Mother felt sad. I'm sure of it. But it's almost like she didn't know how to *do* sad. Not like Aunt Josie did, anyway. Crying wasn't Mother's style, just like wearing slacks wasn't her style.

So instead of getting sad, Mother got mad. A week after the crash, she paid Marvin Kinser from the hardware store thirty dollars to put a lock on her bedroom door. For almost nine months after the crash, I could hear Mother in her room, pacing the hardwood floor and slamming things down hard on her marble-top dresser. That's how mad she was.

At first, I hollered up to her whenever I heard "Swap Line" come on the kitchen radio. I knew she couldn't hear it upstairs. Mother didn't believe in keeping a radio or television in the bedroom. So I'd yell up the stairs: "Swaaaaaap Liiiiiiiine's on! You're gonna miss 'Swap Line.'"

Before the crash, Mother always wanted to know when it was on. That's why I kept hollering up to her. Sometimes I added, "It's a good one!" even though I couldn't hear what was being swapped.

I did that for weeks. I thought listening to her

favorite radio show might cheer her up a little. But she never answered back. Somehow or other Mother had lost interest in hearing about the junk in other people's lives. Maybe because for once we had a fine mess of our own—and not a soul to swap it with.

THREE

A Job to Die For

WHAT YOU REMEMBER FROM FUNERALS are the little things. The tiny details.

The deep scratch in the front-row pew you never noticed because you never sat that far up before.

The geometric patterns that church lights throw on glossy caskets.

The fact that caskets come in different sizes and colors. (Lilac Rose's was pearl white. Wayne Junior's was midnight blue. Daddy's was gray.)

The fact that caskets have handles for carrying.

The way the smell of flowers can make a person sick. Mother told me later that if she smelled one more bouquet of roses, she'd surely vomit.

The embarrassment of having 300 people,

including every teacher in town, looking at your backside. The even worse embarrassment of being seen wearing a calico dress and white gloves. Mother insisted on the gloves because my fingernails were still grimy from replacing my bike chain the week before.

Lilac Rose loved to wear gloves. She liked pretty things. I told Mother she ought to put my sister in her dance recital costume with all the sequins and spangles. That was Lilac Rose's favorite dress. But Mother ignored me and dressed my sister in her white Easter dress and gloves.

She dressed Wayne Junior in his brown corduroy suit. I stared at him all during the funeral, just waiting for him to pop up like a jack-in-the-box and say it was all a joke, like he'd said after her gave me that trick pepper gum that was supposedly cinnamon. But he didn't move.

Neither did Daddy. He was stretched out in his casket wearing a starched Ozark Air Lines uniform. Mother even propped his pilot cap on his head. It was a darn shame his eyes were closed because Daddy had eyes the color of bachelor's buttons.

My brother had the same color eyes, but on him they could look devious on account of all the shenanigans he pulled, most of which involved tricks ordered by mail. Mother was always threatening to send Wayne Junior off to military school if he didn't shape up. But she wasn't serious. The fact was, nobody laughed harder at his pranks than she did.

Of course Mother wasn't laughing at the funeral. She wasn't crying, either. Neither was I.

I knew I should've cried, but I couldn't. I didn't feel sad. That's the other thing about funerals: Sometimes you don't feel sad. You don't feel anything at all other than a sense of floating above yourself and looking down on the scene, thinking: *That's not really me. That's not really them.*

After the service I sat with Mother and Mamaw in the backseat of a fancy black funeral car as we rode from First Baptist Church of Digginsville to the cemetery. Past the Digginsville K–12 School ("Home of the Mighty Moles!"). Past the Dig In Diner. The Donut Hut. The Crossroads Hotel, which was the only three-story building in Digginsville (population 402). Past the Graff twins, Merry and Murray, walking with their fishing poles in the opposite direction down Highway E toward Doc Lake.

A reception was held at our house after the burial. People skulked around, eating lukewarm casseroles off Chinet paper plates and talking about how wonderful my sister, brother, and Daddy all looked in their caskets.

"Wayne has never looked more handsome," declared Mrs. Kay Beth Bowman.

"I heard between the three of them, they had five hundred broken bones," added the dour Mrs. Nanette Toyt. "But to look at them, you'd think they'd just taken a little nap 'stead of fallen out of the sky in Wayne's personal *air-o-plane*."

Where I grew up, lots of people put an *O* in the word *airplane*.

"Thank heaven Hattie wasn't in the plane, too," added Miss Savannah Phifer.

Didn't they know my mother never flew on account of her motion sickness? Even car trips made her queasy.

"Why Wayne needed to have his own *air-o-plane* I'll never know," commented Mrs. Bernette Slick. She had streusel cake crumbs on her cheek. "Do you know how much an *air-o-plane* costs?"

"I betcha Wayne got a discount on it from Ozark Air Lines," murmured the baggy-faced Mr. Bud Mosley. His wrinkled suit was covered with yellow cat hair. Pickles, Mr. Mosley's cat, was probably wandering down Main Street at that very moment, wondering where his bed had disappeared to.

I wondered if Bud Mosley ever found someone interested in his cracked aquarium. *Why didn't he just throw the stupid thing away? If it was cracked, it was broken.*

"Never mind what a plane costs," blurted Mrs. Joetta Porter. "Did you see those curls on little Lilac Rose? She looked like an absolute angel. And Wayne Junior looked like a young prince. Hattie did a *lovely* job."

"Indeed she did," confirmed Mrs. Nanette Toyt. "Those beauty school classes Hattie took before she got married sure paid off. And didn't she look pretty in that navy blue suit? That color complements Hattie's black hair and fair skin so nicely."

"I've *always* said," added Miss Patrice Wood, holding up a thin finger, "that Hattie looks exactly like Ava Gardner."

My mother was pretty, even on the day of the funeral. As for the rest of my family, I thought they looked like wax mannequins. I couldn't understand why, weeks after the funeral, everybody was still talking about how beautiful they looked.

But that's how Mother was hired by Danielson Family Funeral Home as a hair stylist for dead people. She was promised forty-five dollars for every corpse she styled.

"And just think, Daralynn," Mother told me the day she got the job. "I won't have to waste a slim dime on hair spray. A person's hair's not likely to get wind-blown lying in a coffin."

+   +   +

I began to think of my life as a time line. Before the Crash was B.C. After the Deaths was A.D.

In my B.C. life, my mother didn't have a job. Now in the A.D. era, Mother was going to be a hair stylist for dead people.

In my years B.C., I shared a bedroom with Lilac Rose. Now in the A.D. years, I had my own room.

For most of my life B.C., I'd been part of a family of five. Now we were a family of two—just Mother and me, plus Mamaw next door.

My entire life B.C., Mamaw ate dinner with us only on Sundays. Now she ate with us every night. But it never felt like a real dinner because we kept eating off Chinet paper plates. Mother didn't have the energy to wash real dishes, and she didn't trust me with the china.

After the grief casseroles tapered off, Mother lost the will to cook. So we started ordering all our food from the Schwan's man, who delivered frozen food in his refrigerated truck with the built-in compartments. Our weekly Schwan's order consisted mainly of ice cream and Salisbury steak TV dinners.

I hated Salisbury steak TV dinners, both B.C. and A.D. It didn't help that Mother served them with Schwan's heat-and-serve Parker House rolls, which she burned every single solitary night. That's something Mother never would've done B.C.

Something else Mother never would've done: Hired Marvin Kinser to build a breezeway. But that's exactly what she did one month A.D.

It was just a flimsy hallway that connected the den in our house to Mamaw's bedroom. Mother said she wanted to be able to go back and forth to Mamaw's house without going outside, which made zero sense to me.

"What's gonna happen just by walking next door?" I wanted to know.

But Mother didn't answer. She was in her silk bathrobe, watching Perry Mason crack a criminal case on television—yet another thing she'd never done B.C. She's the one who always called TV the "idiot box."

I suspect the real reason Mother had the breezeway built was so she could wear her slippers and robe on days she wasn't working. That's what Mamaw wore, too.

Mamaw's mind started going downhill real fast after the crash. She started forgetting things—simple stuff, like how to address an envelope. Then she started acting downright silly, like she was a little girl instead of an old lady with frizzy gray Albert Einstein hair.

I knew for a fact that Mamaw was losing her mind the day she asked if she could play with my new dolls. When I said no, she began sneaking in my bedroom to steal them.

The first time she did it, I thought: *Good gosh, Lilac Rose and Wayne Junior will DIE when they find out Mamaw's playing with dolls!* And then I caught myself. That was a B.C. thought.

Living in A.D. was going to require a whole new kind of thinking. So I surrendered myself to the unshakable truth that everything had turned terrible, and there was nothing I could do about it.

And with that thought, something inside me turned off with a click.

FOUR

Four Back, Three Under

i HID THE DOLLS under Lilac Rose's twin bed, but Mamaw still managed to find them. She liked to drag a dozen or more dolls down to our living room and talk to them for hours. Most days when I came home from school, she asked me to play dolls with her.

"I don't *like* dolls," I always said.

What I liked was fishing at Doc Lake, but Mother wouldn't let me go there. After the crash, she kept me on a short leash. I wasn't allowed to go anywhere on my own except to school and back.

During Christmas vacation I started bugging Mother to let me go to the funeral home with her. She was preparing for her new career as a hair stylist for corpses.

"I can't have you distracting me," Mother said when I asked the first time.

I was helping her put an electric blanket on my bed. That blanket, a carton of malted milk balls, and the new edition of the *Guinness Book of World Records* were my only Christmas presents that year. (I could tell already that holidays were going to be slim pickings in the A.D. era.)

"I won't distract you," I promised. "I just want to help. You don't have to pay me or anything."

"Who said anything about *paying* you?" Mother replied. "Besides, you don't even brush your own hair. Why would you want to learn how to style other people's hair, especially when they're dead?"

She had a point. Hair had never interested me like it did Mother or Lilac Rose. They could spend an entire Saturday night curling Lilac Rose's hair with Dippity-Do.

"Think about this," I tried again. "What if there's a terrible disaster, and you have a whole bunch of bodies to pretty up? You'd need an assistant. Even Perry Mason on TV has his secretary, Della Street, to help him."

"Humph," she mumbled as she smoothed my bedspread over the lumpy electric blanket.

I followed Mother downstairs. She stopped in front of the thermostat and studied the dial.

"Really, you should *think* about it," I warned darkly. "Something really *big* could happen where you'd need my help."

"Is that a fact?" Mother said without a trace of enthusiasm. She dismissed the notion that I might ever be of help to her as she turned the thermostat down to fifty-eight degrees. Then she turned on the television and waited for Perry Mason to come on and save the day.

+ + +

The next funeral was in the middle of January. To my surprise, Mother let me go with her to help prepare the body for viewing.

It was Carlotta Coldwell, our next-door neighbor on the other side, and the owner of Carlotta's Cute Cuts, the only beauty parlor in Digginsville.

"Everyone'll be looking at Carlotta's hair," Mother said when we arrived at the funeral home. "So it's got to look nice. Just watch closely and you'll see how this is done."

Mother was bossing me as usual, but I knew she was the one who was nervous. This was her first real client and only the fourth dead person she'd ever groomed.

Mrs. Coldwell's thin body was stretched out on a wheeled cot in the basement of Danielson Family Funeral Home. Her eyes were glued shut and she was wearing a plaid wool suit. She looked like a dead bird that somebody thought would be funny to dress up in people clothes.

"All right then," Mother began. She was opening a small aqua suitcase filled with hairbrushes, combs, bobby pins, and curlers. "Most older ladies look good with a little height in their hair. So I'll take these big rollers—you want to use four of them—and, starting an inch or two from the hairline, curl the hair back. Then you take three rollers—one on each side and another in the very front—and curl the hair under, like this."

"Four back, three under," I repeated, watching her work.

"That's right," said Mother. "And you never have to mess with the hair on the back of the head."

"Why not?" I asked.

Mother stopped rolling Mrs. Coldwell's hair and glared at me like I was an idiot. "Because Carlotta'll be lying in a *casket*," she said.

"Oh, yeah. Right."

"Now," Mother said, resuming her rolling, "if this were anybody else, I'd probably have started with a shampoo and blow-dry, and then used some hot rollers. But Carlotta's hair's so brittle from all the years she dyed it, I hate to risk damaging it, especially before her funeral."

"Uh-huh."

"And if this were a gentleman," Mother continued, "he'd likely need a shave and a trim."

I remembered how she'd trimmed Daddy's sideburns that night at the funeral home.

"Just tidying up," Mother said, matter-of-factly. "This isn't the time or place to give someone a completely new hairstyle, though God knows, most people could use it."

She stepped away from the cot and admired Mrs. Coldwell's rolled hair. Then she pulled a tiny pair of scissors from the suitcase and began cutting the flyaway hairs that had escaped the rollers. Mother's face had the same look of calm concentration she'd had when she was curling Lilac Rose's hair and grooming Daddy and Wayne Junior in this room less than three months earlier.

I remembered the hours she'd spent that night,

petting their faces and stroking their hands. Maybe I should've touched them, too. But I couldn't. I couldn't believe that was *them*. I couldn't believe the whole thing had happened. I couldn't do anything but float above myself and watch, just like I was doing right then with poor old Mrs. Coldwell. Big help I'd be to Mother with her new business.

"Now," Mother said, "we have to be sure her fingernails are clipped and clean because she'll be holding a Bible."

"Okay," I said.

Mother leaned down to examine Mrs. Coldwell's nails. Then she frowned. "I better redo Carlotta's manicure. This color she's wearing is way too orangey for the suit she picked out. Daralynn, run home and get my bottle of Pink Blush nail polish."

When I returned, Mother was removing the rollers and teasing Mrs. Coldwell's hair into a big silvery cloud.

"See how easy that was?" she said, clearly pleased with her work. "Four back, three under. That's all you have to remember."

It took me a while to get the hang of it. I had to steal some of my dolls back from Mamaw to practice. But by the time the daffodils started coming up in

Digginsville, I was almost as good as Mother at styling hair. And by that time, she was getting requests from living people to do their hair, too.

That's when Mother decided to open a beauty parlor.

"You should call it Hattie's Hair Hut," I suggested. "Or how 'bout From Cradle to Grave?" I was just trying to be helpful.

But Mother snapped at me. "It's not going to have a name. It's not going to be *that* kind of place." She was sitting at the dining room table surrounded by a pile of unpaid bills.

"What's it going to be then?" I asked cautiously.

"Nothing fancy or showy," stated Mother, who despised anything that could be construed as attention seeking. "Just a place where people can get their hair cut for a reasonable price. That's all."

Mother described her new business as a public service for Digginsville. But even I could see the real reason sitting right there on the dining room table: We needed money to pay our bills.

So with the insurance check she got in the mail, Mother bought Mrs. Coldwell's old beauty parlor. It was just three blocks from our house, right next door to the post office. Without even hanging up a new sign, people began stopping in before or after picking up their mail.

As a hairdresser, Mother was no-nonsense. I suspect some customers appreciated this. Others probably missed the chitchat and gossip that always floated around Mrs. Coldwell's shop.

My mother had never been a gentle touch, but the plane crash combined with her new business of styling corpses reduced her bedside manner to zilch. Occasionally I'd hear an "Ow!" or an "Easy now, Hattie."

"Beg your pardon," Mother always apologized. "I guess I don't know my own strength."

I sure did. Nobody was stronger than my mother. And if a customer tried to console her—even just to say whenever they saw an *air-o-plane* flying overhead, they thought of Daddy—Mother would respond with tense politeness: "Have you ever thought about curling this section of hair right here? It might look better with a little bend."

And that would be that.

Mother paid me a dollar for every head I shampooed. Until school let out, I could work only on Saturdays. Mamaw worked the other days. She liked being useful. And we all liked the fact that the beauty parlor gave us something new to talk about at dinner.

But the air inside our house felt dead, even when we opened the windows.

So when it started getting warm again that first spring A.D., the three of us began sitting outside on our porch after dinner—until the sounds from Aunt Josie's house drove Mother back inside in a rage.

FiVE

Aunt Josie, Purveyor of Sweetness

AUNT JOSIE WAS DADDY'S ONLY SISTER. Her given name was Joanne Cecilia Oakland. When she was eighteen, she had it legally changed to Josie Oakland.

"I wanted something sassier," Aunt Josie told me once when I asked her why.

Sassy. Saucy. Flashy. Trashy. These were some of the words I heard used to describe my aunt. Only my father, Aunt Josie's younger brother, seemed amused rather than offended by her sense of style.

One time, years earlier when we were on our way to a family gathering, I heard Daddy tell Aunt Josie: "Sister, I believe a bird is building a nest in your hair."

"It's a *hat*, Wayne," Aunt Josie corrected. "And it's from New York City, if you must know."

Daddy just laughed. But it was that kind of pronouncement that made me adore Aunt Josie. Truth was, I worshipped her.

Aunt Josie was the self-appointed fashion expert in Digginsville. But her real job—the one she got paid for—was based in her home, a rambling Victorian, four houses down the street from ours.

Her business was called The Summer Sunset Retirement Home for Distinguished Gentlemen. It operated on a trio of related principles:

1) Aunt Josie needed a reliable source of income.

2) There were plenty of old men who had no one to take care of them.

3) Aunt Josie loved men.

She didn't mind cooking or cleaning or even sharing her home with them, provided they made a monthly donation to the house. Aunt Josie didn't charge her *gentlemen*, as she called them, a set fee. They simply gave her what they thought was an appropriate sum for living in the bedrooms scattered on the second and third floors of Aunt Josie's house.

Aunt Josie had a starched white nurse's uniform she wore without the benefit of a nursing degree. Her gentlemen couldn't seem to tell the difference. Neither could most flu bugs.

For more private matters, Uncle Waldo was on hand to help with sponge baths and other matters of personal hygiene. Uncle Waldo was Daddy and Aunt Josie's older brother. He'd been living in the attic of Aunt Josie's house ever since he came back from the Vietnam War six years earlier.

Everyone knew Aunt Josie took good care of her guests. Whereas other old men in Digginsville tended to look raggedy with their tangled gray beards and rumpled clothes, Aunt's Josie's gentlemen were always tidy and clean shaven. They even smelled nice, thanks to the lavender spray Aunt Josie used when she ironed their clothes.

It was no wonder Aunt Josie had a waiting list to get into The Summer Sunset Retirement Home for Distinguished Gentlemen. Her residents were the best advertisement, of course. But she also took out a weekly ad in *The Digginsville Daily Quill.* The ads always said the same thing:

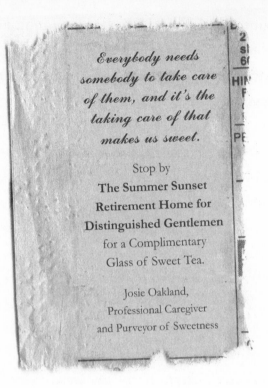

Everybody needs somebody to take care of them, and it's the taking care of that makes us sweet.

Stop by
The Summer Sunset Retirement Home for Distinguished Gentlemen
for a Complimentary Glass of Sweet Tea.

Josie Oakland,
Professional Caregiver
and Purveyor of Sweetness

No question about it, Aunt Josie believed in sweetness. She served her gentlemen dessert after lunch and dinner, and dumped a full cup of sugar in her pitchers of sun tea. (That was the tea she drank, not the stronger tea she used to dye her hair red.)

When the weather warmed up, Aunt Josie liked to spend evenings with her gentlemen on her front porch—or the *veranda*, as she called it. The men listened to the radio while Aunt Josie ironed. She'd cut a hole in her screen door long ago so she could run extension cords from the living room to the porch. That's how she managed to iron and play the radio on her veranda.

"It's a fire hazard," Mother muttered when the music first began wafting down toward our house that first spring after the crash. "Not to mention a public nuisance."

This was an evening in April, not long after Mother opened her beauty parlor. We were on our front porch after dinner. Mother was hemming a flower-print dress while Mamaw was rocking a baby doll. (She'd found the stash of dolls I'd tried to hide from her in the back of my closet.) I was stretched out on the porch swing, digesting another Salisbury steak TV dinner.

"It's not just the music," Mother grumped. "She's got them playing cards and dice games every night."

As if envisioning another family tragedy, Mother reached over from her metal chair and stopped the porch swing with her hand.

"If I *ever* hear of you going down there without my permission," she said, her eyes meeting mine. She didn't have to finish the sentence.

Mother knew how fond I was of Aunt Josie. I admired her flashy way of dressing with those big earrings and talon-like nails, always painted bright red. She was eight years older than Mother, but a hundred times more fun. She's the one who taught me how to play Crazy Eights. She was also one of the few people who didn't bring me a stupid doll after the plane crash. She gave me ten tickets to the Rialto Theatre in Norwood.

"Invite a boy to go see the movies with you," she'd said.

Of course I didn't even bother to ask Mother if I could do such a thing. I knew she'd say no. Some of my best friends were boys, but I wasn't allowed to do things with them—not even go fishing. Mother said sixteen was the age children from good homes began dating. (Never mind that Wayne Junior had been taking girls on swimming dates to Doc Lake since he was fourteen. I knew because I followed him.)

Mother was still grousing about Aunt Josie and her music that spring evening when the devil herself came sashaying down the street from her house, her long red hair bouncing to the beat of her high heels clicking on the sidewalk.

"Hattie, I think it's flat-out *fantabulous* that you've

taken over Carlotta's beauty parlor," Aunt Josie hollered up to Mother from the base of our porch steps.

Mother didn't respond.

"And I know you're doing a bang-up job," Aunt Josie continued. "*Everyone's* talking about it. I'm going to have to come down there myself and get a summer cut. You think you can squeeze me in?"

Mother finally deigned to respond. "Sorry, Josie," she said, holding a hand up to her ear. "I'm having a hard time hearing you with all that noise coming from your house."

Aunt Josie laughed. "Frank Sinatra is not *noise*. He's music. And my gentlemen just *love* listening to music."

Mother smiled sourly in Aunt Josie's direction. Compared to her tarty sister-in-law, my mother looked like a church organist with her jet-black hair pulled back into the tight knot she always wore at the base of her thin neck. She evil-eyed the extra flesh escaping from Aunt Josie's catalog-ordered dress as if to say, *See? That right there is what eating dessert twice a day does to a woman's body!*

"And how's your sweet mother this fine evening?" Aunt Josie asked in her soothing voice. "My goodness, you look fresh as a daisy in that housecoat."

Mamaw looked across the porch for guidance. Mother nodded, as if granting a child permission to speak.

"I'm fine, thank you," Mamaw offered tentatively.

"And how 'bout you, Miss Daralynn?" Aunt Josie hollered. "You found yourself a boyfriend yet?"

Mother cast a lethal look my way.

"No ma'am," I responded, my entire body ablaze with embarrassment.

"Good for you!" Aunt Josie cheered, pushing a tumble of red curls over one shoulder. "Be a career girl, like me."

It wasn't the response I expected from Aunt Josie. Then again, nothing Aunt Josie said or did was predictable.

"Say, Hattie," Aunt Josie called. "What do think about planting some purple coneflowers around the gravestone? I think that'd look real pretty, don't you?"

Mother didn't answer. We hadn't been to the cemetery since the day of the funeral. That was fine with me. Seeing that stone with all their names on it would make it seem final. Permanent. Set in stone.

"Black-eyed Susans would be pretty, too," Aunt Josie said from the sidewalk.

Silence. Mother's eyes were fixed on her sewing.

"Okay, then. Have a good evening, y'all," Aunt Josie hollered as she turned to walk back toward her end of the block. And then she added: "Oh, and Hattie, I *am* coming in for that haircut. I want you to give me a real stylish look for summer, okay?"

"When you-know-what freezes over," Mother muttered under her breath.

SiX

Let Dolly Do Your Hair

I HAD ALWAYS BEEN A GOOD STUDENT in the B.C. era. In fifth grade, I even won the American Legion contest for an essay I wrote about patriotism.

But in those first months A.D., I had the hardest time concentrating. I could read the same sentence ten times without getting its meaning. The words wouldn't stay still on the page. And when I tried to do math, the numbers just danced around on my paper.

My mind was in a fog. It was like I was underwater in Doc Lake and didn't have the energy to come up for air. When school finally let out for summer, I was glad.

My grades didn't suffer too horribly bad, thanks to my sixth-grade teacher, Mrs. Staniss. She was also my fifth-grade teacher. After the crash, whenever she called on me to give a homework answer, I'd say something like: "Uh, sorry, I didn't get that one." And right away she'd say: "Don't you worry one little bit, Dolly. Say no more."

(Mrs. Staniss, wherever you are, I will always be grateful to you.)

Even when she gave me my report card on the last day of school, she put her hands on my shoulders and bent down to talk to me, face-to-face.

"What you went through last fall was a *trauma*," Mrs. Staniss said gently. "Do you know what that means?"

"Yes ma'am," I said.

Mrs. Staniss stared, as if waiting for me to elaborate.

"Er, I mean, no ma'am," I amended.

"What it means," she said carefully, "is that it could take a long time for you to feel like *you* again."

"Right," I said. I didn't tell her that I'd been thinking I might never feel like me again. I felt tired and a thousand years old. It didn't help that all the girls in my class had stopped calling me for sleepovers and bike rides way back before Christmas. Even the boys ignored me. It was like they all thought they might catch death from me, like you catch lice from a comb you find in the alley.

"I know this has been a long school year for you, Dolly," Mrs. Staniss continued. "You know what you oughta do this summer?"

"What?"

"Take it easy," she said. "Get some books out of the library. Or take your fishing pole down to Doc Lake." She paused before adding: "Just tell your mother where you're going."

Seven months after the crash, everybody in Digginsville knew the reason I wasn't in Daddy's plane when it crashed. Because I'd been grounded for going fishing without Mother's permission.

"Fishing sounds real good," I lied. I didn't tell Mrs. Staniss how low my expectations were for summer. It was just another way that life A.D. was different from life B.C. Back then, the promise of summer always made me feel like an explorer ready to set sail for a new, uncharted continent. Now, summer felt like a school field trip to some place I had no interest in going.

"Or, wait a second," Mrs. Staniss said. She started

digging through her desk drawers. "I know what you should do this summer."

She pulled a thick red book from a bottom drawer and handed it to me. The words PERTINENT FACTS & IMPORTANT INFORMATION were embossed in gold on the leatherette cover.

"Someone gave this to me for Christmas," she whispered. "But I think it's a better gift for you."

"Uh-huh," I said, trying to look grateful as I thumbed through the blank pages.

"You can use it for anything," Mrs. Staniss said brightly. "Write stories in it. Or keep a diary. You've always been a good writer, Dolly. This summer you should write. Write about, you know, everything."

"Thank you," I said. "I'll try to do that."

Of course, Mother had other plans for me.

"Except when I'm preparing a body for viewing, I'll be at the beauty parlor," she told me one hour after my conversation with Mrs. Staniss. "So you can spend your summer there with me and Mamaw."

It would've been one thing if I could've made a little walking-around money by being Mother's full-time shampooer. But Mamaw had claimed that job for herself. She loved shampooing customers, and they loved her right back.

"Jesus take me now," they'd say when Mamaw was giving a shampoo. "I feel like I've died and gone to heaven."

"There, there," Mamaw would coo in response. "Be a good baby and close your eyes." To Mamaw, everyone had become a baby doll.

By the time school let out, all of Mother's customers were requesting shampoos by Mamaw, which left me nothing to do but thumb through boring old housewife magazines with articles like "Fowl Play: 30 Chicken Recipes That'll Make Your Family Cluck with Pleasure!"

The only bright spot in those early summer days was when a customer came in with a kid or two. Back then, nobody had babysitters, at least not during the daytime. Any woman with children under the age of thirteen generally brought them with her to the beauty parlor.

Carlotta Coldwell always kept a refrigerator stocked with soda pop for kids. As with Aunt Josie's business, there was no set price. Customers simply dropped a handful of change in the glass jar labeled POP MONEY before opening the fridge and grabbing a cold Fanta or Coca-Cola.

I convinced Mother to continue this tradition.

"It'll be good for business," I told her. Little did I know that my first business would be born one day while drinking a root beer from Mrs. Coldwell's old fridge.

It was the afternoon Flora Denison, a classmate, came in with her mother. I was drinking a root beer. Flora bought an orange Fanta and slumped in the chair next to me and my stack of housewife magazines.

"Don't you hate when you have to run errands with 'em all day long?" Flora asked. She was in the same boat as me.

"Yup," I said, sipping my root beer through a tiny straw. I was trying to make it last. Mother allowed me only two sodas per day. "And it looks like your mom's getting her hair permed and frosted. You'll be here for two hours at least."

Flora made an unattractive sound as she slurped her orange soda. Mother glared at me from across the room.

"Hey, want me to do your hair in a French twist while you wait?" I asked Flora. I was trying to save us both.

"You know how to do a French twist?" Flora said, perking up.

"Yeah," I answered. "I got so bored last week, I read all of Mrs. Coldwell's hairstyling books."

I didn't tell Flora what I'd discovered: that fixing hair wasn't all that different from tying fishing lures.

When I finished, Flora couldn't take her eyes off her reflection in the mirror. Before the week ended, girls were coming to the beauty shop with and without their mothers, asking me to braid their hair and trim their bangs. Some brought pictures from magazines and begged me to make them look like famous actresses. Faye Dunaway and Julie Christie were popular requests.

And then boys starting coming in with baseball cards, asking me to cut their hair like Johnny Bench and Catfish Hunter.

"Let Dolly do your hair!" all the kids began saying. So that's what I called my salon, which was just a metal stool with a swivel top in the back of Mother's shop. I hung a curtain from the ceiling to separate my side from hers. I also found a mirror and made a sign with pictures of hairstyles I liked glued on poster board. Mother said I couldn't charge more than one dollar a head. So that's what I did.

I won't claim that I was a born beautician. I had my share of disasters, starting with the time Barry

Howe came in on the first hot day in June. Barry was a boy in Wayne Junior's class.

"My cousin Frankie from Iowa's spending the summer with us," Barry said, gesturing with his head to the young relative at his side. "Have you got time for a haircut while I deliver groceries for Mr. Swisher?"

"Sure," I said, patting my metal stool and eying cousin Frankie, who had the scruffiest mop top I'd ever seen. The poor kid's hair was worse than the rock 'n' roll wig Wayne Junior wore for Halloween when he was in eighth grade.

"It's a shame to hide a good-looking face," I told Frankie, repeating what I'd heard Mother tell her customers. And then I twirled the stool around and started cutting.

A trick I learned from Mother was to turn customers so they faced away from the mirror while you cut. That way you avoided any unwanted audience participation. And if you did a good job, you could really wow them when you finished.

Well, I thought I did a nice enough job on Barry Howe's cousin. But when I spun him around on the stool to reveal his new cut, the dang kid burst into tears.

Why? Because it turned out cousin Frankie was

a *she*. And I'd just given her my best Marlon Brando haircut.

"I look like a boy!" Frankie shrieked.

"No, no, no," I said, stalling so I could think up an excuse. "Maybe folks in Iowa don't read fashion magazines. But good gosh, don't you know this is the most popular style in France this summer? Why, yes it is! It's just as stylish as can be."

After Barry Howe returned and escorted his sniffling cousin out the door, Mother pulled the curtain aside and gave me an exasperated look.

"Shoes," she finally said.

"What?"

"If you don't know whether your customer's male or female, look at their shoes."

"All right," I said.

"And if you *still* don't know, for heaven's sake, ask *me*." And she yanked the curtain closed.

I grabbed my scissors and looked in the mirror. Then I took aim. Mother must've heard me because she pulled the curtain back again.

"Now what are you doing?" she asked. "Daralynn, *stop* that! *Stop!"*

But I kept going.

"Daralynn!" Mother hollered when she saw big

hunks of hair falling from my head. "What on God's green earth are you doing?"

"I'm giving myself the same haircut," I reported glumly. And that's exactly what I did.

Lilac Rose would've been horrified if she could've seen the results. Wayne Junior would've laughed himself sick. But I think Daddy would've understood. He always said how important it was to follow the Golden Rule. If doing unto others as you'd want them to do unto you was the rule, then doing unto my stupid self as I'd stupidly done unto somebody else seemed only right.

I left the beauty parlor that day looking like a rat terrier in cutoff shorts.

SEVEN

Our New Neighbor

WE FIRST HEARD THE NEWS from Miriam Throckmorton. She was married to Dallas Throckmorton,
the local real estate agent.

"Well, I think it's just as sweet as can be that your
brother-in-law wants to live next door to you," Miriam announced to Mother on the second Monday in
June.

"What?" Mother said. She'd been combing out
Miriam's freshly shampooed hair, but this news
stopped her cold.

"Haven't you heard?" Miriam chirped. "He'll be
living right next door to you."

"In Mamaw's house?" I asked from my side of the
curtain.

I was sitting on my stool, staring in the mirror and trying to see if I could force my hair to grow by tugging on the roots, like I'd seen Mamaw do with my Beautiful Crissy dolls.

"Not in my house," added Mamaw. She was shampooing Mrs. Kay Beth Bowman.

"No," Miriam Throckmorton said. "On the other side. Waldo's bought Carlotta Coldwell's old house." Then, turning to Mother, she added in a loud whisper: "He told Dallas he wants to get *closer* to you."

Mother said nothing.

"Well, he's never married, has he?" Mrs. Kay Beth Bowman contributed from the shampoo tub. "Unlike Josie, who's married and divorced . . . Well, how many times has it been? Does anybody even know?"

I knew. Aunt Josie had been married five times, judging from the wedding pictures she kept on her mantel. But I didn't say anything.

"And Waldo's a certified war hero," Miriam Throckmorton added. "Of course he paid the price for it. But who didn't?"

Uncle Waldo had been a pilot, like Daddy. But he didn't work for Ozark Air Lines. Uncle Waldo was a fighter pilot in the Vietnam War. He didn't fly anymore, though. Daddy said something happened to Uncle Waldo in Vietnam that made him act nervous and a little on edge. I often wondered what exactly was wrong with Uncle Waldo, but the details were fuzzy.

"I must say," Miriam Throckmorton yammered on, "as tragic as Wayne's passing was in that terrible, *terrible* plane crash, you have to wonder if maybe it wasn't God's plan to get you and his brother Waldo togeth—OWWW!"

"Oh," Mother said flatly. "I hope I'm not combing too hard."

I knew what Mother was really hoping: that Miriam Throckmorton had her facts wrong. But the information was correct. When we got home from the beauty parlor that afternoon, we found Uncle Waldo pulling weeds in Mrs. Coldwell's old perennial garden.

He smiled shyly. "Josie hasn't kicked me out, if that's what you're thinking."

Mother crossed her arms and stared at his bald head. Uncle Waldo had been unencumbered by hair for as long as I could remember. Wayne Junior used to call him Uncle *Baldo* until Daddy told him to be respectful.

"I've admired this house a long time," Uncle Waldo said, looking at his hands. "I don't know if Carlotta ever told you, but I asked her to sell this place to me a dozen times. She was too old to be living alone, and I'd hoped, well . . ."

Uncle Waldo cleared his throat nervously. He could see Mother's eyes narrowing. I felt a bit sorry for him, as one victim of Mother to another. Something about Uncle Waldo always reminded me of those sad-looking dogs that wear barrels around their necks.

"What I was thinking," attempted Uncle Waldo, dropping his head even lower, "is that we might build a breezeway and connect our houses. That way, if you ever needed anything—any little thing, day or night—you could just holler through the breezeway and I'd come over and do whatever you—"

"One breezeway is quite enough, thank you," Mother said, lifting her chin with pride.

"Oh yes, I know you had Marvin connect your house to your mother's after the, uh, you know, the accident," Uncle Waldo stammered. Then he spoke in a quieter voice. "But let's be honest. Taking care of the elderly isn't easy. I know how hard it is, believe me. That's why I thought I could help you on this side. You know, by fixing things. Doing odds and ends." He coughed airlessly. "I hope you don't mind that I've noticed the spring on your screen door could use a little oil. If you want it to stop squeaking, I mean."

"I apologize if my door has disturbed you," Mother said in her iciest voice. "I'll add it to Marvin's to-do list."

"Oh, I didn't mean that," Uncle Waldo put in quickly. "I just meant that, well, I'm fairly handy, you know. And I'd be happy to help out around your house any way that I could. It wouldn't have to be anything more than that. But in time, if you discover you enjoy my company and want to—"

"Daralynn," Mother said, "take Mamaw inside. *Now.*"

It was only then that I realized Uncle Waldo was quite possibly courting Mother.

She joined us in the house a few minutes later.

"Is Uncle Waldo going to *live* with us?" I asked.

"No," Mother said gruffly. "But I can't stop him from buying a house if he has the money."

She was mad, that's for sure. And she was even madder when he came to the beauty parlor a few days later.

"Even bald men need a little upkeep now and then," Uncle Waldo said.

"Not much I can do to help you there," Mother said without looking at him. She was sweeping hair clippings off the floor. Ribbons of blond hair mixed with clumps of gray and black curls.

"Hattie," Uncle Waldo said, "I was thinking about planting some rosebushes around the gravestone. But I wanted to make sure that was okay with you."

Mother just kept sweeping. I knew she was thinking what I was thinking: the smell of all those roses at the funeral. It really was enough to make a person sick.

Uncle Waldo smiled. "Okay, I'll hold off on that," he said. Then he bought a root beer for me and a grape soda for himself. He stuck a five-dollar bill in the jar and left.

"No reason to be rude, Hattie," Mamaw said after Uncle Waldo was gone.

"You can count the hairs on that man's head with one hand," Mother said, dumping a dustpan full of hair into the garbage. "One *finger*, even."

"A baby can't help it if he's bald," said Mamaw, rinsing out the shampoo sink.

But to Mother, baldness was a sign of moral failing, like crabgrass and dandelions.

"And then he has to *show off* by overpaying for those soda pops," Mother hissed. "I swear, he's just like his sister."

She said it like it was the worst possible thing you could say about a person. But it made me look at Uncle Waldo in a new, more favorable light. Or maybe I just felt sorry for anyone foolish enough to try to be sweet to my mother.

EiGHT

Clem's Crematorium

LATER THAT WEEK AN UNFAMILIAR car was spotted cruising through town. A man no one knew was seen pounding wooden stakes in the empty field where the Digginsville Dairy Dream had been before it burned down.

A few days later, a hand-painted sign stood in the middle of the staked-off area. The sign read FUTURE HOME OF CLEM'S CREMATORIUM. I thought it meant we were getting a new Dairy Dream—and just six blocks from my house.

"Are you excited about the new crematorium?" I asked Janelle Harper. She'd come in the beauty shop for *Le Frenchie,* as everyone was calling the Marlon Brando–inspired haircut I'd given Barry Howe's cousin Frankie. All the girls in Digginsville suddenly wanted *Le Frenchie* cuts after they heard—and believed—it was the hottest hairstyle in France.

I was just trying to make small talk while I thinned the hair around Janelle's ears. But it was obvious from her reaction that I'd hit on a sore subject.

"No, I'm *not* excited," she said without hesitation. "I'm absolutely *disgusted.* Imagine someone you love dying and then being *burned* up till they're just a pile of ashes."

"What's that got to do with hot-fudge sundaes?" I asked.

Janelle turned the stool around with her feet so she could stare me down in the mirror. "Dolly," she said in a superior tone, "you don't honestly think a crematorium is an *ice-cream parlor,* do you?"

Honestly I did. But I was too proud to admit my ignorance.

"I bet *you* don't know what it is, either," I said.

"I most certainly do," Janelle replied with confidence. "A crematorium is a place where bodies get cremated."

"Cremated—like *burned?*"

"Ashes to ashes, dust to dust," Janelle whispered solemnly. "Isn't it just the creepiest thing *ever?*"

She swatted away a comma-shaped clump of hair that had fallen onto her lips. Janelle had been a mouth breather since kindergarten. It made cutting her hair a challenge.

"If you ask me," I said, "being buried in the cemetery doesn't exactly sound like a barrel of laughs."

"Yes," said Janelle. "But at least if you're buried, your family can come visit you and decorate your grave on Memorial Day."

Memorial Day. Wasn't that in May? Right after school let out? This was June. I didn't tell Janelle that Mother and I had neglected to decorate our family's gravestone. It was none of her dang business.

"Whereas if you're cremated," Janelle continued, "there's nothing to visit. You're just a sad little pile of dust that blows away and is forgotten forever by everybody."

She shuddered and left. At least she remembered to pay me a dollar for the haircut. I stuffed the bill in the coffee can with the rest of my college money.

It turned out my other customers all felt the same way as Janelle about the crematorium. That is, until the following week when Aunt Josie came in for *Le Frenchie.* (Mother still refused to cut her hair.)

To my surprise, Aunt Josie was in favor of the new

crematorium, which turned out to be a trailer house with white vinyl siding and green plastic shutters.

"'Course it's a little tacky to look at," Aunt Josie conceded. Years ago she'd hired some high school kids to paint her house a lively shade of lavender. Over time the color had faded considerably, like Aunt Josie herself.

"But no, I don't mind having a crematorium in town," she said. "Most of my gentlemen don't have family around here. Being cremated means they can have someone like me scatter their ashes wherever they want to go. Eureka Springs. The Grand Canyon. Even Timbuktu, if that's what they want."

I had a hard time picturing all this. "How do they do it?" I asked. "Do they just throw the bodies on a brush pile and then rake up the ashes?"

"Heavens no, child," crowed Aunt Josie, her eyes closed tight as I chopped her wild mane of red hair. "It's all very scientific. I've met Mr. Clem and he's awful smart. He told me about this machine he has. It takes care of everything in a very professional manner."

"But what about the viewing of the body?" I said. "Don't people like to get one last look at a person so they can say good-bye?"

I was thinking back again to that night in the funeral home when Mother was curling Lilac Rose's hair and trimming Daddy's whiskers and Wayne Junior's hair. I was wishing I'd done a better job saying good-bye instead of just standing there, doing nothing.

"There are some people who think it's morbid to dress up a dead body," Aunt Josie explained. "Besides, when a person dies, you should celebrate their life, not mope around about their death."

This made sense to me.

"When it's my time," Aunt Josie went on, "I want you to get out all my scrapbooks and find the most flattering pictures of me. Put them in pretty frames on tables all over my house. And then I want you to invite everyone over and throw a big old party."

"A party?" I asked. "At your house?"

"That's right," she instructed, her velvety voice rising. "Serve Bubble Up and club sandwiches, and let people stay as long as they want. And then, a week or so later when everybody's gone, scatter my ashes in the backyard. Just sprinkle them under the apple tree."

"You want to be *cremated*?" I asked, shocked.

"Sure," she said. "Why not? It's how the old-timey Greeks and Romans did it. It's just a *body*.

Truth is, I don't care what you do with me as long as you don't bury me underground. I've never been a stick in the mud, and I don't plan to start being one when I'm—"

"You about finished over there, Daralynn?" Mother asked from her side of the curtain. "Because you've got two cases of Coca-Cola that need to be put in the fridge."

Aunt Josie looked at me and shrugged.

When I finished cutting her hair, Aunt Josie was so pleased with her new look, she gave me a ten-dollar bill.

"It's only a dollar," I said, handing back her money.

"Shush," she said, shaking her newly shorn head. "Child, you *earned* it. Don't I look like Mia Farrow? And if I'm not mistaken, I've just lost five pounds—in hair."

She admired her reflection in the mirror for several minutes. Then she turned and looked over her shoulder, admiring herself with puckered lips and a "come hither" expression. She laughed and gave me a big hug before pulling the curtain and walking toward the door.

"Bye for now, Hattie," Aunt Josie said, leaning in

to give her sister-in-law a hug. But Mother flinched and successfully dodged the embrace.

It was a snub, to be sure. But I could tell what my mother was thinking just from the look in her eye: *Josie looks pretty even with her head practically scalped! Ack!!*

Of course I was thinking something else entirely. *Someday Aunt Josie won't be around anymore. And there's not one darn thing I can do about it.*

NiNE

Putting the *Fun* Back in Funeral

I HAD SUSPECTED MOTHER WAS OPPOSED to the crematorium just because Aunt Josie was for it. But that wasn't the problem at all.

"That crematorium is going to put the funeral home out of business," Mother told Mamaw one night when they were sitting on the porch. It was after dinner. I was in the living room, eating a jelly sandwich and listening through the screen door.

"Just a matter of time," Mother explained. She was combing out a pile of artificial hairpieces she used on customers with thinning hair. "Dan Danielson said cremation is the way of the future. If the funeral home goes out of business, I'll lose my best customers—the dead ones who don't complain. And then I'll lose all my *living* customers who want to look snazzy on funeral days."

She was right to worry. The days leading up to a funeral were always the busiest days in a small-town beauty parlor.

Mother was still grumbling about the crematorium when the sound of music from Aunt Josie's house floated through the trees and down to our house.

"That *woman*," Mother snarled.

"Baby likes her music," murmured Mamaw, washing a Barbie doll's hair in a roasting pan. Mamaw had become so forgetful with names she'd started calling everyone Baby. Yet her ability to ferret out my dolls—even after I hid them under the basement stairs—was uncanny and impressive.

"The way she carries on with those *men* of hers," Mother elaborated. "I swear."

But just then, I heard the voice of a man who didn't sound old enough to be one of Aunt Josie's boarders. He had a deep, distinguished voice like a doctor on a TV show. When the song ended, the trill of Aunt Josie's laughter filled the air. Minutes later, she and the man with the deep voice were walking in front of our house.

"Oh, Mr. Clem," Aunt Josie purred. "You shoulda been a *comedian.*"

"Please," replied the male voice. "Call me Clem."

Mother blasted through the front door. "I cannot be*lieve* Josie's been entertaining a *cremator* in her house," she fumed. She stopped when she saw me. "Daralynn!"

I thought for sure I was going to get in trouble for eating in the living room. "I'm being care—" I started to explain.

"Hush!" Mother ordered. Then she hid behind the door so she could listen to the conversation on the sidewalk without being seen. I listened, too.

"Now Mr. Clem—er, Clem—" Aunt Josie was saying, "I want you to use Old Mary any time you want. I keep the key in the ignition, so you just help yourself. Don't even bother askin' because I'll just say take it. It's yours for the borrowing."

"Not even her truck," Mother whispered behind the door.

This wasn't entirely true. Daddy had given his 1959 Ford F-100 pickup truck to Aunt Josie after Mother complained that it was an embarrassment to have a rusty pickup parked in our driveway. Aunt Josie named the truck Old Mary. She used it to get her Christmas tree every year and also to haul junk to the dump whenever she cleaned out her garage. She even let me drive Old Mary up and down her driveway a couple of times when Daddy said it was okay.

"Daddy gave her that truck," I whispered.

"Shhhh!" Mother said, erasing away this fact with a wave of her hand. She leaned in closer to the screen door. I followed suit.

"Why, Miss Josie," Mr. Clem was saying, "I'm beginning to see why you're the most popular lady in Digginsville."

Mother emitted a deep growl as she spun away from the door. "Put Mamaw to bed," she directed me. Then she retreated upstairs to her bedroom, where I heard the unmistakable sound of delicate things being slammed on a marble-top dresser all night long.

+   +   +

It was my idea to put the *fun* back in funeral. After sleeping on the problem, I told Mother and Mamaw my thoughts the next morning at breakfast.

"I've heard some folks like to celebrate the life of a person who's passed, rather than their death," I began.

Mother stared at me as she stirred her coffee. The altitude of her eyebrows told me she knew exactly where I'd heard this.

"So I was thinking," I said, "what if you talked the funeral home into offering living funerals? It'd be a way to—"

"*Living* funerals?" Mother asked. "That's a contradiction in terms."

"Let her finish," Mamaw said. "Go on, Baby."

I hadn't really thought the whole thing through yet. But I just kept talking while Mother glared at me, and Mamaw held a glass of orange juice to a doll's plastic mouth. I was hiding those dolls all over the house, but Mamaw always managed to find them.

"Well," I ventured, "what if the funeral home offered people a chance to have a little get-together before they die? It'd be like going to your own funeral, but you'd be *alive* so you could hear all the nice things people generally say about dead people. And you'd get to thank the people in your life who—"

Now it was Mamaw who cut me off. "Funerals upset my babies," she said, putting the doll over her shoulder to burp.

But Mother was smiling. "This is good," she said. "This could work."

And then she dumped her coffee in the sink and marched over to Dan Danielson's house to tell him the idea.

The following Monday, this ad ran in *The Digginsville Daily Quill*:

We're Putting the "FUN" Back in Funeral!

Don't wait till you're dead to celebrate your life. Book your LIVING FUNERAL now and be the LIFE of the party—not the death.

Living Funerals are available *only* at Danielson Family Funeral Home.

TEN

The Life of the Party

Aunt Josie's *Le Frenchie* hadn't grown out even a smidgen, but she was back on my swivel stool the day after the ad appeared in the newspaper.

"What's all this about *living funerals?*" she asked in her quietest voice, which was as loud as most people's regular speaking voice. Mother was humming church hymns on the other side of the curtain.

"You're the one who gave me the idea," I whispered directly into her ear.

"*Me?* What do you mean?" Aunt Josie wanted to know. "You're going to put my Clem out of business."

"Your Clem?" I said, pretending to cut the back of her hair. There was nothing left to cut.

"We're planning to get married after he gets the crematorium up and running," Aunt Josie stated in a hushed voice. "But I'm afraid this living funeral business could ruin everything."

"Sorry. I'm just trying to help Mother."

"I know you are, child. Do you think it's gonna work?"

"They've got one booked already," I admitted.

"A living funeral? *Who?*"

"Uncle Waldo," I said.

Aunt Josie spun around on the stool. "*My* brother's having a living funeral?"

"He's sending out invitations. I'm sure you'll get one."

"An invitation to a *funeral*," she said, shaking her head.

I showed her the tasteful card I'd received in that morning's mail.

You're Invited to
Celebrate the
Life and Times

of Waldo Emerson Oakland

at my
Living Funeral
Saturday, June 28
8 to 10 o'clock in the evening
Danielson Family Funeral Home
(No gifts, please.)

"Well, I'll be ding danged," Aunt Josie declared.

+   +   +

Mother and I helped Mr. Danielson decorate the viewing room with streamers and balloons. We used one of the display caskets as a buffet table, setting plates of cucumber sandwiches on top of the polished wood. My job was ladling out limeade-sherbet punch from Mother's cut-glass punch bowl.

At Uncle Waldo's insistence, Mr. Danielson agreed to play dance records instead of the usual fake classical music. And sure enough, a half hour into the living funeral, guests started pushing chairs to the side of the room. A dance floor was born.

"Never in all my days did I think I'd see people dancing in the viewing room," Mr. Danielson told me.

Uncle Waldo wore a pressed brown suit. He greeted guests in his usual shy manner. I noticed the only person he wasn't nervous around was his sister.

"I should've done this years ago," he told Aunt Josie at the punch bowl. "I've talked to more people tonight than in all the years since I moved back here."

"Goody gumdrops for you," Aunt Josie said sarcastically.

Uncle Waldo laughed. "You're just mad your new boyfriend wouldn't come with you. Is that it?"

"No, that's *not* it," Aunt Josie protested. "If you must know, I've already been to one brother's funeral. I wasn't planning on going to another's so soon."

Uncle Waldo slung his arm around Aunt Josie's shoulder. "Relax," he said. "I'm not going anywhere. That's the whole point of a living funeral. I'm celebrating the fact that I'm *alive*, not dead."

"Oh," Aunt Josie said, more quietly than before. "Well, okay then."

Minutes later Aunt Josie was on the dance floor,

teaching everyone the steps to a new dance called the Hustle. Uncle Waldo was telling people he might die laughing.

Before the night was over, six people had spoken with Dan Danielson about booking living funerals. My idea had worked! Besides keeping Danielson Family Funeral Home afloat, living funerals would double the number of events on the Digginsville social calendar, meaning women would need to get their hair done twice as often as usual.

"I owe you," Mother told me that night as we walked home from the funeral home. "Just tell me what you want, and I'll get it for you."

"It's okay," I said. "I don't really need anything."

That was a lie. There was something I did need, but I didn't know how to ask for it. It wasn't exactly something you could buy in a store.

"Think of something," Mother said. "I need to compensate you for your idea." Then she laughed. "*That'll* teach Josie to try to steal my business."

"Aunt Josie wasn't trying to steal anyone's business," I said.

"Of *course* she was," Mother countered. "She and that ridiculous new boyfriend of hers."

"Aunt Josie says she and Mr. Clem are getting

married," I said. I felt a twinge of guilt for sharing this news without permission.

"Married?" Mother snorted. "That'll be the day."

My mother had always been rough, tough, and hard to bluff. But now she was getting just plain mean. It wasn't only the things she said. It was the hateful way she said them and the underlying assumptions, like doubting Mr. Clem would want to marry Aunt Josie.

As we walked in silence, I thought about what I really wanted. I wanted to talk about Lilac Rose, Wayne Junior, and Daddy. I wanted to remind Mother how funny we always thought it was when Daddy used to call home and say he and his flight crew were grounded by Mother Nature. I'd tell him that I was grounded by Mother. That was one of our favorite jokes in the days B.C., back when we had family jokes.

I remembered how we all used to listen to "Swap Line" and laugh every time Daddy threatened to call in and try to swap his three kids for a goat. I wanted to ask Mother if she remembered that. I wanted to ask if she thought Daddy and Wayne Junior and Lilac Rose would've liked having living funerals.

I bet Lilac Rose would've loved it. She would've invited the whole town and put on a fashion show, complete with different hairdos to match her favorite outfits. Maybe she'd even do a little tap dancing if she could remember her routine from last year's recital. And then she'd thank everybody in town for making her life possible, like she was a Hollywood actress winning an Academy Award.

Wayne Junior would've made a joke out of his living funeral. He'd have invited all the boys from his class. They'd wear ball caps and sit around making rude noises with their hands and armpits.

I tried to imagine what Daddy's living funeral would've been like. It was hard to picture it. He wasn't much for crowds, and he never talked about his feelings. The only time Daddy ever used the word *love* was when he sent us postcards. Anytime he was gone for more than two days, he sent us a postcard. Of course, he usually managed to beat his postcards home. (Mail delivery was notoriously slow in Digginsville.) But that didn't matter. It was just fun to get something in the mail, especially something that said, "Love, Daddy."

Maybe Daddy's living funeral would've just been a quiet little ceremony with him giving everybody he loved a postcard with a note written especially for that person. Wouldn't that be a nice thing to have?

I wanted to ask Mother if Daddy left her anything

sweet like that. Did he leave me anything? Did he really want to swap us all for a goat?

I could get lost in memories of my family. But then I realized it was all getting farther and farther away. Already I couldn't remember the smell of Lilac Rose's favorite bubble bath. I couldn't even remember exactly what Wayne Junior's trick pepper gum tasted like—except bad.

If I could forget these things, did it mean I could forget them? Earlier in the week when I'd been bored at the beauty shop, I'd tried to sketch Daddy's face on the back of a magazine. I was shocked to discover I couldn't remember what side he parted his hair on. I ran home and looked in the photo album, where the images were still clear—unlike my memory, which was getting fuzzier by the day.

I wanted to know if Mother was ever going to talk about them again. Or was she trying to forget them? Was that it? And then there were the darker questions that had been rattling around in my brain for the past eight months: *Did Mother wish she'd been killed in the plane crash so she wouldn't have to be stuck here with me? Or did she wish I'd been killed along with the rest of them so she could start over from scratch?*

That's what I really wanted to know. Those were

the questions that had been bugging me like two rocks in my shoe since the funeral. But I couldn't ask for those answers. So I asked for something easier.

"How 'bout a root beer float?" I said.

"All right," Mother said. "That's easy enough."

But when we got home, we found we were out of both vanilla ice cream and root beer.

"That man they have driving for Schwan's is a blithering *idiot!*" Mother yelled, slamming the freezer door with a solid *thwunk.*

"Doesn't matter," I said. And the truth was, it really didn't. It's not what I wanted, anyway.

Two hours later I was lying in bed when I felt a low vibration coming from outside my window. I got up to look. It was Old Mary, gliding past our house toward Aunt Josie's.

I stayed at the window long enough to see a man in a dark suit a few minutes later. He was walking by our house. He was alone. I couldn't see his face in the darkness, but I knew who it was. He walked just like he sounded.

"Hey there, Mr. Clem!" I yelled out the window. He turned to look, but I chickened out and squatted to the floor. *What was I thinking?*

I stayed crouched low for several minutes. When

I finally inched my head up again to look out the window, Mr. Clem was gone. But the night air had changed. I felt goose bumps on my arms. My heart began beating faster.

I rummaged under my bed and found the book Mrs. Staniss had given me on the last day of school. I wiped a thin layer of dust off the red leatherette cover and admired the official words: PERTINENT FACTS & IMPORTANT INFORMATION. Then I opened the book to the first page. With a thin black marker, I started writing:

Dear Daddy, Wayne Junior, and Lilac Rose,

A lot has happened since you've been gone, which I can fill you in on later. Right now I want to tell you about a man named Clem who's moved to town. I think you'd find him mighty interesting.

That first letter I wrote was fourteen pages long. And I was just getting warmed up.

ELEVEN

Mother Gets Really Mad

MOTHER ALMOST SPIT OUT HER coffee when she opened *The Digginsville Daily Quill* the next morning and saw the ad on page three:

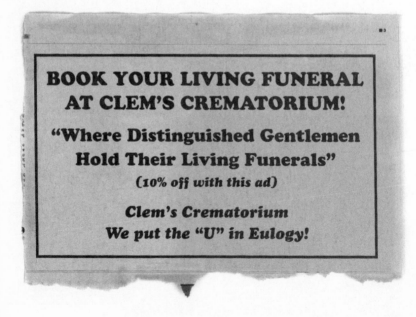

BOOK YOUR LIVING FUNERAL AT CLEM'S CREMATORIUM!

"Where Distinguished Gentlemen Hold Their Living Funerals"
(10% off with this ad)

Clem's Crematorium
We put the "U" in Eulogy!

"That contemptible woman!" Mother said, flinging the newspaper down on the kitchen table.

"What's wrong?" asked Mamaw. She was in the living room, holding a tea party for a few of my dolls, which she'd found under the sofa.

"They stole our idea," Mother said, standing up from the table. "It was *our* idea, and now they've stolen it."

"Who?" I asked. I was scraping off the burnt portions from the toast Mother had made me.

"Josie and her *despicable* boyfriend, that devil!" Mother bellowed.

She started pacing the kitchen floor. Then she stopped, picked up the telephone book, and shuffled through the pages. She dialed a number.

"Hello, Avis?" she said. "Hattie Oakland here. Fine, thank you. I'm sorry to bother you at home on a Sunday morning, but I've just opened the morning paper and . . . Yes, it always arrives by seven o'clock. Thank you. But the reason I'm calling, Avis, is the advertisement you've placed on page three of the paper."

She paused. I hadn't eaten a bite of toast since Mother dialed. Even Mamaw stopped playing with the dolls to listen.

"It's for living funerals at Clem's Crematorium,"

Mother explained. "As you surely know, Avis, that's something new and *unique* that we're offering at Danielson Family Funeral Home. For you to take money from some *interloper* who's not even *from* here, someone who just comes to town and *steals* our ideas *and* our business. Well, how would you like it if someone from another—"

Avis Brown—owner, publisher, editor, and only reporter for the local newspaper—was obviously trying to get a word in edgewise. Mother closed her eyes and listened briefly before exploding again.

"No, Avis, I *don't* see your point," she snarled. "Free enterprise? No, I do *not* look at it that way. What? No. I hadn't heard that. Good-bye, Avis. You can cancel my subscription to *The Quill*."

She hung up the phone and wiped the sweat from her forehead with the back of her hand. It wasn't even eight o'clock and already the air was heavy. That was what summer felt like in the Ozarks.

"Did you know there's already been one cremation in this town?" Mother asked grudgingly. She was plunking ice cubes in her coffee.

"Who?" I asked.

"We didn't know her," Mother replied. "She was from California. Killed in a car accident on Highway

60 a few nights ago. The family wanted her cremated. Avis said it was very '*ecological*.'"

Mother said the word *ecological* like it was a swear word. I didn't have the nerve to remind her how often Daddy had talked about the importance of being mindful of our natural resources. He was always getting on Lilac Rose about wasting food and leaving lights on. He taught Wayne Junior how to measure the air pressure in the car tires so we'd get more miles out of a tank of gas. He even taught me how to measure the air in my bike tires so I could conserve my own energy.

I liked thinking back to the old days. But then I remembered the larger issue at hand. A cremation meant no viewing of the body, which meant no customer for Mother, which meant forty-five dollars down the drain.

"Get ready for church," Mother said. "We leave in half an hour."

All through church I thought about our new competition in the living funeral business. It was obvious that Aunt Josie was involved. But why? Couldn't she see we needed the money? I knew Mother's pride would never allow her to admit such a thing to Aunt Josie. It was up to me to save Mother's business.

During Preacher Bradford's sermon, I began to strategize how I'd go about doing it. I needed more information. Somehow I had to sneak down to Aunt Josie's house and talk to her privately so I could find out who Mr. Clem was, and why Aunt Josie had fallen for him so fast.

"Mother," I said, walking home from church in the sticky heat, "since we couldn't make root beer floats last night, can I have something else?"

"Huhn," she grunted. She was still spinning over that ad.

"Can I go fishing instead?" I asked.

Sunday afternoon fishing was something Daddy and I used to do. We'd start talking about it on the way home from church: deciding what kind of bait we'd use and what might be biting. Afternoons are never the best time for fishing, of course. If you want to catch fish, you go in the early morning or at dusk.

But fishing isn't always about fish. Daddy and I never cared if we caught anything or not. We just liked being outside. Daddy always said he got his best thinking done when he fished. That's when he said he solved all of life's problems. I just liked getting out from under my mother's thumb, which was exactly what I wanted to do right then.

"I haven't been fishing in a long time," I reminded Mother.

"Don't be gone long," she said, her mind clearly elsewhere. "And eat something before you go."

I ran the rest of the way home and changed into my cutoff shorts and an old T-shirt. After stuffing a fistful of Ritz crackers in my mouth, I retrieved my fishing pole and Daddy's tackle box from the basement. I assumed Daddy's fishing gear belonged to me. Mother surely wouldn't want it. Still, it felt a little funny to take it without his permission.

"Bye!" I yelled as I raced out the back door. The screen door screeched and slammed behind me.

"Looks like somebody's going fishing."

It was Uncle Waldo. He was standing in his backyard with a man in a pale yellow suit.

"Daralynn," said Uncle Waldo, "have you met Mr. Clem Monroe?"

TWELVE

What This Town Needs . . .

i WAS SURPRISED TO SEE he didn't look like the devil.

Clem was quite handsome with his shiny black hair parted in the middle and a black mustache that curled up on the ends, like the jack of spades. His sparkling green eyes twinkled in the late morning sun. And when he opened his mouth to smile, you could see he had the whitest teeth in the whole county. Daddy would've said Clem stood out like an orchid in a dandelion patch.

I set my fishing gear down in the grass so I could shake the hand that was reaching over the wooden fence in search of mine.

"Clem Monroe," he said, smiling.

"I'm Daralynn Oakland," I said. "Some people call me Dolly."

I knew I should apologize for yelling at him from my bedroom window, but I didn't know how to bring it up. Maybe he hadn't heard me.

"My pleasure to meet you," he said grandly. "But why didn't anyone tell me there's a fishing spot in this charming hamlet?"

"Are you a fisherman?" Uncle Waldo asked. He was checking the oil in Mrs. Coldwell's old lawn mower.

"You better believe it," Clem answered. "Canada. Minnesota. Key West, Florida. Now *there's* some good fishing."

Uncle Waldo laughed. "Clem won't find anything like that around here, will he, Daralynn?"

"No sir," I answered. "But if you like catfish, we've got plenty of them in Doc Lake."

"Doc Lake?" Clem asked. "I'm intrigued."

"Don't be," said Uncle Waldo. " 'Doc' is short for Department of Conservation. The lake was dug out by state conservationists years ago. They keep it stocked with largemouth bass and channel catfish. A few bluegill, I suppose."

"Where is this lake?" Clem asked. "And how big is it?"

"Fifteen acres," I answered. I'd done a report on it in second grade. "Doc Lake's not far from here. Just a mile or so out Highway E."

"And you're *walking* there?" Clem said. He looked either impressed or distressed. I wasn't sure which.

"I can't very well ride my bike with all my fishing stuff," I explained. "If you're in a big hurry, there's a shortcut through the woods. But you'll get eaten alive by chiggers and ticks."

I hoped like heck he wasn't going to offer me a ride. Mother would turn a triple backflip if she found out I'd accepted a ride from Mr. Clem. She would flip if she knew I was even talking to him.

"Is there no public transportation in Digginsville?" Clem asked.

"We're a little small for a subway system," Uncle Waldo said with a smile. "Or even a bus."

"Right," said Clem. "And city buses would detract from the rustic charm of the town. Mmmm."

I watched Clem stroke his mustache with his thumb and index finger. Then, suddenly, he clapped his hands loudly.

"I've got it!" he announced. "What this town needs is a horse and carriage."

"A *what?*" said Uncle Waldo.

"A horse and carriage," Clem repeated. "So people wouldn't have to walk everywhere."

Uncle Waldo laughed.

"I'm serious," Clem said. "It breaks my heart to see a sweet little girl walking a mile each way in this heat." He turned to look at me. "Wouldn't it be more fun to hop on a horse-drawn carriage and *ride* to the lake?"

"Sure!" I said.

And then I felt a spasm of guilt in my stomach when I remembered this was the man I'd decided to start investigating. Maybe he was as nice as he seemed. He certainly was a creative thinker.

"New York City has horse-drawn carriages," Clem elaborated in a professorial tone. "New Orleans, too. But they're strictly for tourists. Here, it could serve as a legitimate form of transportation." He took a breath and rubbed his chin thoughtfully. "In a town this size, the simplest route would do. Even I could design it. The carriage would stop at eight or ten places around town. The hotel. The diner. The donut shop.

Post office. Grocery store. Doc Lake. And it'd be free for passengers."

"Who's going to pay for these pony rides of yours?" Uncle Waldo asked, still tinkering with the mower.

"The state has money just sitting around for *exactly* this sort of thing," Clem insisted. "Same with the feds. I'm sure business owners in town would kick in some money. It'd be a service for their customers, especially the older folks who can't get around as easily."

I could imagine what Mother would say if Mr. Clem asked her to help pay for a horse and carriage.

"Do you think your mother would mind if I mowed your backyard?" Uncle Waldo asked as if reading my mind.

"Only if she found out," I replied.

Cutting the grass had always been Wayne Junior's job. Ever since spring, Mother had tried to hire high school boys to help with yard work. But as they never mowed to her satisfaction, she'd taken over cutting the front yard with a rusty old push mower from the garage. She couldn't get the gas mower started, so she didn't bother with the backyard, which had become a jungly mess.

Uncle Waldo pulled the choke and started Mrs. Coldwell's old lawn mower with a roar. I picked up my fishing gear with one hand and waved to Mr. Clem and Uncle Waldo with the other. Then I ran down the alley, straight to Aunt Josie's house.

THiRTEEN

Uncle Clem?

AUNT JOSIE WAS IN HER backyard, pinching suckers off tomato plants. I couldn't help thinking of Wayne Junior, and how much he loved tomato and peanut butter sandwiches.

"Daralynn!" Aunt Josie hollered musically. "Come talk to me. Tell me who was at church and what they were wearing."

I told her as best as I could remember. Truth was, I'd spent most of the service thinking about how Clem had stolen our idea for living funerals, and wondering if Aunt Josie was involved.

"Are you helping Mr. Clem sell living funerals over at the crematorium?" I asked, getting right to the heart of the matter, like Perry Mason did on TV when questioning a witness.

"I am," confirmed Aunt Josie. "And would you believe we've got one booked already? Mr. Aubrey Bryant's throwing his living funeral next Friday afternoon, after the Fourth of July parade. One o'clock at Uncle Clem's crematorium. But come over at twelve thirty so you can—"

"*Uncle* Clem?" I interrupted.

"Well, child, he's *practically* your uncle," Aunt Josie said with a theatrical wave of her hand. "We're getting married just as soon as he gets the crematorium up and running."

I noticed that the polish on Aunt Josie's nails was chipped. This was new for her.

"Oh, I know I'm behind on my manicures," she admitted when she saw me staring at her hands. "I just haven't had time for that lately, what with marketing the crematorium and taking care of Clem and all my other gentlemen. But I will, honey, once I get my ring."

"Is Mr. Clem living here with you now?" I asked.

"Heavens, no," Aunt Josie said. "That wouldn't be proper. He's staying over at the hotel. He just comes down here for meals. Someone's got to take care of that man before he works himself to death."

We both laughed.

"He *better* not die on me," Aunt Josie said. "Not before he pays me back the money I loaned him. I don't know how the cremating machine works. And I don't *want* to know." She leaned in closer and continued in a hushed voice: "I've had nightmares about getting locked in the crematorium and being burned alive."

"What's it look like?" I asked.

"The cremating machine?" Aunt Josie said, returning to her tomatoes. "I wouldn't know. I've not seen it. Clem has to keep it locked up tighter than a drum. Regulations and all that."

I started pulling weeds at the other end of the tomato bed. "Did you know Mr. Clem's talking about getting a horse and carriage for Digginsville?" I asked.

Aunt Josie laughed. "I'm not surprised. Not one bit. I've never met a man who had so many brilliant ideas. He's a genius. And he's the handsomest man this town has ever seen. Besides your father, that is."

I thought my daddy was ten times more handsome,

but I didn't mention it. Instead, I asked, "Do you love Mr. Clem?"

"I do," Aunt Josie said without hesitation. "I know it all seems sorta sudden, but when it's right, you know it."

"How?" I asked.

That really made Aunt Josie laugh. She had a big, husky laugh that seemed to come from somewhere deep inside. Then she turned surprisingly serious. "It's not something you can explain in words," she said slowly. "It's just something you know. Emotions can catch you by surprise. They can sneak up on you. That's the best way to fall in love."

Lately I'd been wanting to ask Mother about her courting days with Daddy. (Those Rialto movie tickets were burning a hole in my pocket.) But like a lot of things, I sensed she wouldn't like talking about romance and such things now.

"Is that how Daddy and Mother fell in love?" I asked Aunt Josie. "Did their emotions sneak up on them?"

"You better believe it," she said. "I remember when your father met Hattie. He called me the morning after their first date."

"What'd he say?"

"He said he'd met the girl he intended to marry. He said Hattie was the smartest, prettiest, sweetest girl in town."

"Mother—*sweet?*"

"She *was* sweet," Aunt Josie said. "Even to me."

"You'd never know that now," I grumped.

"Daralynn, think about it. Can you imagine losing your husband *and* two children? 'Course you can't because you don't have a husband or children. Me neither. But it's been hard on your mama. It's hardened her heart, like it would anyone's. That's why I don't take the things she says to me personally."

"You don't?" I asked.

"Heavens, no," Aunt Josie said, swatting away the notion like it was a mosquito. "It's not about me. It's about *her.* You think I can't hear her *tirading* against me when I play my music in the evenings? But I play it loud so she can hear it, too. The woman needs some music in her life. She needs love."

"She can be hateful at times," I said, yanking a thistle from the tomato bed.

"I know she can," Aunt Josie agreed. "But that's what keeps her going. Being mad is what keeps her from being sad. If she weren't mad, your mama might just lie down and die of sadness. I don't think she's even had a good cry yet, has she? Lord, I don't think I've *ever* seen Hattie cry."

"She doesn't cry," I reported. "Or laugh."

Of course, I hadn't been doing much of those things, either. But I didn't mention that part.

"The person in this town who needs a living funeral is your mother," Aunt Josie stated. "But she's the last person on earth who'd ever have one. Emotions embarrass her. And she hates people paying her any kind of attention. Look at poor Waldo. He would marry Hattie in a heartbeat."

"She doesn't like bald men," I said apologetically.

"That's an excuse," Aunt Josie said. "Your mother's afraid to love. And after what she's been through, I don't blame her."

"You think she's going to be like this forever?" I asked.

" 'Fraid so," Aunt Josie said, shaking her head. "Unless she finds someone she feels like taking care of."

"That person better have good hair," I said.

Aunt Josie cackled. Then she wrapped her arms around me and squeezed me tight. "This is what keeps me grounded," she said, rocking me from side to side.

"*Grounded?*" I said. My voice was muffled because I was smushed up against Aunt Josie's ample bosom. "Grounding's what Mother used to do to punish me."

"Not that kind of grounded," Aunt Josie said. She unwrapped her arms and pointed to the big apple tree in the corner of her backyard. "Grounded like a tree. What keeps that tree standing up straight?"

"The roots?" I said. "The sun? Dirt? I don't know."

"All of it," she said, taking my hand and holding it. "And most of it we can't even see. But look at the way the earth just hugs that tree. That's what your mama needs."

"A tree—or a hug by the earth?"

"No, child. Somebody to take care of. That's what makes us sweet and keeps us grounded."

In the distance, I heard the church bell ring twelve times.

"I gotta get a move on," Aunt Josie said. "Clem gets hungry as a lion at noon."

She strutted toward the back door in her high

heels and turned around to holler: "Being in love can be a pain in the rump at times, Daralynn. But it's awful fun. You gotta try it sometime!"

I waved. Then I picked up my fishing gear and set off for Doc Lake.

FOURTEEN

Fishing for Trouble

It took me fifteen minutes or more to walk there. I was just strolling along, taking my time and thinking about my investigation.

When I got to Doc Lake, I found a nice shady spot where I baited my hook and cast off. I hadn't been fishing for ten minutes when I heard a car pull up in the gravel parking lot next to the lake. It was Mr. Clem, driving a yellow Cadillac convertible.

"So this is the famous Doc Lake," he yelled in my direction as he got out of the car.

I suddenly felt embarrassed for my town and our sorry excuse for a lake.

"It's not much to look at," I hollered back. Then I turned my head and spit out the piece of grass I'd been chewing. I didn't want him to think I was a complete hick.

"On the contrary," said Clem, smiling widely. "I'd say it's the perfect fishing spot."

He was walking toward me, stepping carefully to avoid getting his dress shoes dirty. He held his hands in his pockets. I could hear coins jingling as he got closer.

"Hope you don't mind me joining you," he said. "I couldn't resist driving out here after my noon-day meal."

"I don't mind," I said. "You want to, um, borrow my fishing pole?"

He laughed. "You're generous to offer. Maybe another time. I really just wanted to see what the drive out here was like. Dare I tell you how easily I can imagine a horse-drawn carriage on Highway E, bringing you and a handful of friends out here to fish?"

"Or swim!" I added enthusiastically. I was getting in the spirit of this horse-and-buggy idea.

Clem's eyes flashed. "Swim? Is there a lifeguard here? I don't see a lifeguard stand."

"There isn't one," I admitted. "We're really not supposed to swim here. See?" I pointed with my pole to the wooden sign attached to a buoy in the lake. The faded letters said:

ABSOLUTELY
<u>NO</u> SWIMMING ALLOWED
NO EXCEPTIONS!

"Oh," he said, squinting at the sign. "I'm assuming that's strictly enforced."

For some reason I couldn't remember what the word *enforced* meant. My brain got tangled up when I was nervous. And here I was talking to a cremator!

"Most kids don't swim here on account of it being so muddy," I said. "But sometimes on really hot days, you can't help yourself."

Clem shook his head and sighed sadly. "More children die every year in swimming accidents than you can imagine. A lot of them at places just like this. If you'd seen what I've seen in my business, you'd think twice about swimming in a lake."

My heart started thumping fast, like it did the night before when I saw him from my bedroom window. "Tell me," I said. "About the stuff you've seen."

"Oh, I can't do that," he said, looking at the sky.

"No, really," I insisted. "I can handle it. Practically my whole family died last fall. It wasn't a swimming accident, but . . . it doesn't matter. They're dead. I can take it. Just tell me, please."

Slowly and with what I interpreted as grave reluctance, he began a formal recitation.

"Necks broken after diving into shallow water. I had several of those in Illinois."

"Go on," I said softly.

"A girl trapped under a canoe. Her friends thought she was hiding from them when, in fact, she was drowning. They were teenagers, drinking beer and roughhousing."

"More," I whispered.

"A young boy swinging from a rope into a lake accidentally strangled himself." He stopped. "I shouldn't be telling you these things."

"It's fine," I said. And I meant it. This was exactly the stuff I needed for my investigation. Plus, I'll admit that it was strangely comforting to meet someone who knew more about death than I did. To me it was still a waxy mystery.

"I hope I haven't upset you," he said.

"Nah," I said, acting cool as a cucumber. "Besides, I don't really even *like* swimming here, anyway. My brother did, but I don't. The fish bite."

Mr. Clem smiled. "You're a good girl. Just be careful, okay?" Then he walked back to his car and drove away.

I continued fishing for the rest of the afternoon. I was nowhere closer to saving Mother's business than I'd been before I'd started my investigation. In fact, it was just the opposite: I was more confused than ever about Mr. Clem.

But then I remembered what Daddy used to say about thinking. He claimed the brain works best when you stop thinking and start fishing.

And just then I got a bite.

I reeled it in slowly. It was a beautiful channel catfish with iridescent gills that sparkled in the sunlight like jewels. Probably a five-pounder, I thought. Big enough to eat, but I didn't like to kill fish. Neither did Daddy. We'd always operated on a catch-and-release policy.

I gently removed the hook. As I did, I saw that the fish had something small and white in its mouth. It fell out on the grass as I tossed the fish back in the lake.

It was a tooth. A human tooth. I threw it in the tackle box and walked home.

That night after dinner (Salisbury steak TV dinners and burnt Parker House rolls—again), I took my *Pertinent Facts & Important Information* book out to the front porch and began to write another letter.

Dear Daddy, Wayne Junior, and Lilac Rose,

Well, I have lots to tell you about an investigation I've started on that fella named Clem I wrote you about last night. But first I want to say that I used Daddy's tackle box today. I'm guessing you don't need it where you are, Daddy, but I wanted to let you know. Anyway, I didn't catch much today. Just a catfish that had a tooth in its mouth. A human tooth! Can you imagine some unlucky fisherman losing a tooth while trying to open a beer bottle?

I wrote for more than an hour that night, mostly about Clem and the things he told me. I ended the letter like this:

P.S. Mr. Clem says swimming in lakes is very dangerous and only foolish teenagers do it. What do you make of that, Wayne Junior? (Don't worry. I won't rat you out to Mother.)

FiFTEEN

Parade of Fools

THE ANNUAL FOURTH OF JULY PARADE was always a big deal in Digginsville. Kids decorated their bikes with crepe paper and rode down Main Street and around the little cluster of side streets we called the neighborhood. Members of troops, clubs, and associations carried banners made from bedsheets and marched behind the bike riders. Anyone with a fancy car drove it behind the marchers.

When I came downstairs for breakfast that Fourth of July, I found Mamaw in our kitchen. She had filled Lilac Rose's old baby carriage with my dolls and was feeding them breakfast.

"The babies are going to be in the parade," she announced.

I stared at my grandmother. She was still in her nightgown. Her hair looked like a gray tumbleweed.

"Have you told Mother you're doing this?" I asked a little meanly.

"*I'm* the mama," Mamaw said sulkily, stroking a life-size baby doll and pressing a Cheerio to its red plastic lips.

This was a disaster! How had she even reached the dolls off the high shelves in the basement where I'd hidden them the night before?

"I'd sure hate to see those pretty babies get run over by a fire truck," I said. "You remember how the fire truck always drives by at the very end of the parade, don't you?"

Mamaw bit her bottom lip. "I don't like when my babies get hurt," she said sadly.

Mother came into the kitchen. She was wearing a sleeveless white dress with a belt that made her look thin as a broom handle. She'd gotten even skinnier since the crash.

"Park the carriage in the breezeway," she ordered. "Babies aren't allowed at the parade. Too dangerous for them. Now go get dressed."

Mamaw did as she was told. Her brain was

turning to mush, but even she recognized the futility of disobeying Mother.

Shortly before ten o'clock, we went outside. Uncle Waldo was standing in front of his house with a coffee cup in one hand and a small American flag in the other.

"Happy Fourth, neighbors," he said, raising a friendly toast to us with his cup.

"Same to you," Mother replied, turning to look in the opposite direction, toward the bike riders two blocks away. "Daralynn, bring a chair down off the porch for Mamaw."

"Let me do that," Uncle Waldo offered, starting toward our porch.

"Daralynn's perfectly capable," Mother said.

I retrieved the chair, planting it in the grass for Mamaw. She always loved a parade.

"Here come the baby bicycle riders!" Mamaw cheered.

A ragtag brigade of fifteen or twenty kids—mostly younger than me—rode their Schwinns in a procession past our house. I sat on the curb and waved mechanically, remembering how much it'd meant to me to see Wayne Junior and his friends waving when I rode in the parade.

After the bicyclists came the local Girl Scout troop, led by Miss Jackie Harris. They were followed by the Boy Scouts (BE PREPARED, DIGGINSVILLE, their banner ominously commanded), the Future Farmers of America, the 4-H'ers, the American Legion, and The Summer Sunset Retirement Home for Distinguished Gentlemen. These were Aunt Josie's five housemates, shuffling along at a glacial pace with their banner held in front of them. Every few steps, one of the men mustered the energy to wave. I waved back, wondering why Aunt Josie wasn't marching with her gentlemen like she usually did.

The antique cars and trucks were next. All the usual suspects were in attendance: Norm Olsen, the mechanic, in the souped-up Mustang he drove once a year. Marvin Kinser from the hardware store in his pickup truck with the chicken-wire Liberty Bell in the bed along with a tape recorder playing a warbled rendition of "It's a Grand Old Flag." And as always, Avis Brown in her shiny white Oldsmobile, throwing tiny packages of red and black licorice with the words WHAT'S BLACK AND WHITE AND READ ALL OVER? THE DIGGINSVILLE DAILY QUILL! printed on the front.

I was surprised to see Clem's yellow convertible behind Avis. He was wearing a jaunty plaid cap and throwing great gobs of saltwater taffy. Aunt Josie pranced alongside the car, passing out leaflets.

I didn't dare try to catch any of Clem's taffy—not with Mother standing twelve inches away. But I couldn't resist seeing what Aunt Josie was up to. When she got close, I stood up and held out my hand.

"Clem says *you're* the one who gave him the idea for this," Aunt Josie said to me in a stage whisper. She was crackling with energy as she handed me a leaflet. I read the words in one nervous gulp.

<u>Giddyup and Give a Buck</u>
<u>for the Digginsville Horse and Carriage!</u>

Wouldn't it be <u>FUN</u> to have a <u>HORSE AND CARRIAGE</u> right here in Digginsville?
Wouldn't it be <u>WONDERFUL</u> to <u>RIDE in STYLE</u>
to your destination rather than walk or drive a car?
If you're interested in bringing a horse and carriage to Digginsville,
please see Clem Monroe.
Mr. Monroe will be collecting donations
from businesses and private individuals.
Let's bring a HORSE AND CARRIAGE to Digginsville!

(When you talk to Clem, don't forget to ask about booking your LIVING FUNERAL at Clem's Crematorium.)

As soon as Aunt Josie had passed, Mother grabbed the paper from my hands and read it.

"A parade of *fools* is what this is," Mother said, crumpling the leaflet and stuffing it back in my hand. She turned her back on the parade. "Come on, Mamaw. We're going."

"Can I get an ice-cream cone?" I asked cautiously. The tradition in Digginsville was that after the parade, everyone gathered at the Dig In Diner for free ice cream. Mother was mad, but she'd let me go fishing by myself. I was hoping maybe she was letting up a bit on my leash.

"Get one and come right home," Mother commanded.

"Thanks!"

I took the alley and ran down to the Dig In Diner, beating most of the parade by several blocks. But news of the horse and carriage had already reached the diner.

"Best idea I've heard in years," Mrs. Eliza Ravinwoods was saying when I walked in the door. "With a horse and carriage, we'll be the envy of the Ozarks. I'm in for fifty dollars."

Mr. Forest Swisher agreed. "Just think how nice a carriage would be for our senior citizens," he said. "They'll be able to do their own grocery shopping.

And I won't have to hire high school boys to deliver groceries. This carriage could save me a bundle. I'm gonna give that Clem fella a hundred dollars."

I thought of Wayne Junior, and how he was planning to buy a car with the money he'd saved from delivering groceries for Mr. Swisher. Then I remembered how Lilac Rose and her best friend, Natalie Jean, were scheming to ask Mr. Swisher if they could be the first delivery girls when they got old enough to work. I wondered how they'd feel about all this.

I stood in line for my ice-cream cone and watched the Summer Sunset men hobble in the door with Aunt Josie behind them.

"Daralynn, honey!" she called with a big wave when she saw me. "You haven't forgotten about Mr. Aubrey Bryant's living funeral, have you? It starts in an hour, but come on over to the crematorium right after you finish your cone. It's going to be packed tighter'n a can of sardines."

"Mother needs me at home this afternoon," I fudged.

"But you'll miss all the fun," Aunt Josie said, clearly disappointed. "It's going to be a terrific party." She turned to address her housemates. "Aren't we all going to have a *good* time this afternoon?"

The old men mumbled weakly in the affirmative.

"Let's get each of you an ice-cream cone, shall we?" she said in her silky voice. "Then we'll have Mr. Clem drive us over to Mr. Bryant's party. Won't that be fun? Did you see Mr. Clem's yellow Cadillac? It's fancy dancy. I just *know* you're going to love riding in it. It's not quite big enough to hold us all so we'll have to go in two shifts. But first, let's get us some ice cream. Mr. Bryant, you go first because it's your big day. What kind would you like? Let's see. They've got chocolate ripple, butter pecan, peach..."

When I left the Dig In Diner with my cone, I could hear Aunt Josie herding her gentlemen to the first living funeral at Clem's Crematorium.

"Won't it be handy when we have a horse and carriage and can travel together?" Aunt Josie was saying. "Mr. Clem says a deluxe carriage can seat six adults comfortably. Won't that be *something*?"

That night as I watched the fireworks over Doc Lake, I thought about Mr. Clem and his horse and carriage. It would be the biggest thing ever to happen in Digginsville. Parades were all well and good, but every town had a Fourth of July parade. Fireworks, too. What other small town had a horse and carriage you could ride in to go fishing?

This would be as big as the Traveling Reptile Museum that rolled into town once a year. The TRM, as it was called, was a ghastly snake show that traveled the country in an air-conditioned trailer, pausing for a few hours on town squares. Folks paid fifty cents for the pleasure of climbing inside the trailer and eyeballing the giant snakes that slithered around on sticks stuck in dusty aquariums.

But we couldn't claim the TRM as our own. It just passed through Digginsville every summer. A horse and carriage would be one hundred times better. It would change the way people lived and went about their business. And I'd get credit (and maybe even a trophy!) for inspiring Mr. Clem with the idea. Of course, he'd be Uncle Clem by then. And who knows? Maybe he'd teach me how to drive the horses—as long as Mother didn't find out. She still thought Clem was the devil incarnate for opening his crematorium.

I decided that night to spend the next afternoon at the public library, researching cremation. I made a list of questions, including: *Why do some people bury dead bodies and others burn them? How did cremation get started? Is it illegal? Is it immoral? What happens to people when they die?*

Before I went to bed, I glued the Giddyup and Give a Buck leaflet in my book of *Pertinent Facts & Important*

Information. Then I wrote another letter to Daddy, Wayne Junior, and Lilac Rose. I ended the letter this way:

Sometimes I wonder if maybe I should call off my investigation of Mr. Clem, especially in light of his big plans for Digginsville, not to mention Aunt Josie's fond feelings for him. But it's almost like I can't help myself. Lilac Rose, remember that time you had poison ivy and Mother told you a MILLION TIMES not to scratch it, but you just couldn't help yourself? That's what this feels like.

Folks are giving him $50 and $100 without blinking. Even Aunt Josie loaned him money. I don't know what I'm expecting Mr. Clem to do next, but it seems that he's doing it at every turn. He's like that two-headed snake in the Traveling Reptile Museum, and all you can do is wait and watch to see what he does next.

Well, I'll fill you in on everything in my next letter.

Love,

Daralynn

P.S. I keep forgetting to tell you all about
this thing I invented called a Living Funeral.
The idea's really catching on. People seem
to like the idea of celebrating life before
they die. It's a way to say nice things to
important people in your life before you—or
they—die.

That night I had a dream about getting a postcard from Daddy. It was addressed just to me, which
never happened in real life. Daddy always addressed
his postcards to The Oakland Family. In my dream I
was so happy to get that postcard, I was flying!

The only bad part was that the postcard was written in a language I didn't understand. And I couldn't
find anyone to read it to me.

SiXTEEN

Aubrey Bryant Leaves a Legacy

WEIRDLY ENOUGH, MR. AUBREY BRYANT died three days later.

"I can scarcely believe it," Aunt Josie whispered. She'd called me at the beauty parlor. It was obvious she'd been crying.

"He hadn't even gone to his ball game yet this summer, had he?" I asked quietly into the phone.

Mr. Bryant's claim to fame was that every year he took the Greyhound bus by himself up to St. Louis for a Cardinals' baseball game. He was one of Aunt Josie's more energetic gentlemen.

"No," Aunt Josie said, sniffling. "Didn't even get to go to his ball game."

"How'd he die?" I asked. But before I could hear the answer, Mother grabbed the phone from me.

"*Who* died?" she barked into the phone.

I couldn't hear Aunt Josie, but I could guess from Mother where the conversation was going.

"And you're going to let him be *cremated*, are you?" Mother said. "All right then. Do as you will." She hung up the phone without saying good-bye.

"Mother," I leaped in recklessly, "*lots* of folks are cremated these days. Maybe not in Digginsville, but in big cities where there's not enough room to bury everyone."

(The *Encyclopedia Britannica* had been very informative.)

"It's not a crime," I added.

"Well, it *should* be," Mother stated. Her face was red and squished with anger. "Jesus told us to care for the dead, not to *burn* them. Cremation is pagan. It's an insult to God. A body can't be resurrected if it's not buried in God's holy earth."

"Not everybody feels that way," I reported. "In some religions, they believe embalming, like they do over at the funeral home, is an abuse of the corpse."

"*Who* believes that?" Mother demanded.

"Uh, I can't remember," I said, backing down. I

was pretty sure it was Jewish people and Muslims, but that wasn't going to help this argument any.

"Christian people burn trash, not bodies," Mother said in her best lecturing voice.

I knew what she was thinking. This was the second cremation in Digginsville, but the first of anyone we'd known. Maybe cremation really was the way of the future.

"At least Mr. Bryant had a nice life over at Aunt Josie's," I said.

No response from Mother.

"I bet he left Aunt Josie a little pocket change," I said in a singsongy voice, knowing this would elicit a response.

"*That* you can be sure of," Mother snorted. The discussion ended when her next customer arrived for a tint and perm.

Everyone knew the tradition at The Summer Sunset Retirement Home for Distinguished Gentlemen. Residents paid whatever they felt appropriate for lodging and meals at Aunt Josie's. And when they died, they were expected to leave a "legacy," otherwise known as a generous donation.

That's why when you visited Aunt Josie's house, you'd see little brass rectangles with words like: WE

ARE INDEBTED TO MR. JAMES ELLSWORTH FOR THIS COM-
FORTABLE READING CHAIR. Or, THIS BOOKCASE WOULD
NOT BE POSSIBLE WITHOUT THE GENEROUS SUPPORT OF
MR. ROBERT FAYEHART AND MR. ARTHUR JOE RAY. Or,
BATHROOM RENOVATION FUNDED BY A HANDSOME DO-
NATION BY MR. BRUCE LYNN PRATER.

Not every legacy donation resulted in a brass
plaque. Some were spent on general repairs for the
house. Others went toward upkeep of Aunt Josie herself in the form of clothes, shoes, hats, and makeup.

Sure enough, the Friday after Mr. Aubrey Bryant's
death, I saw Aunt Josie on my way to Swisher's Grocery. She was wearing a tight-fitting lime green pant-
suit with matching shoes.

"Looks like you got yourself a new outfit, Aunt
Josie," I said, putting my box of empty soda bottles
down on the sidewalk.

"This ensemble," she said in a serious voice, "was
brought to you by an untimely contribution from
Mr. Aubrey Bryant."

I couldn't help noticing that despite the new
clothes, Aunt Josie looked frazzled and exhausted.

"Here," she said, sticking two packs of Black Jack
gum in the pocket of my shorts. "I'm feeling generous. Can you visit a minute?"

We sat down on a bench outside the grocery store. I tore into my gum and was admiring the deep licorice flavor before I realized Aunt Josie was crying.

"Tell me the truth," she said, slumping over with her head in her hands. "Do you think the excitement was too much for him?"

"Do what?" I asked.

"Mr. Aubrey Bryant," Aunt Josie said. "If that living funeral drove him to an early death, I will never forgive myself."

I told her I couldn't imagine how a party could kill somebody. "Besides, he was awful old," I added. "What'd the doctor say?"

"The cause of death was listed as heart failure," Aunt Josie said, blotting her eyes with an embroidered handkerchief. "Dr. Colyer said poor Aubrey's heart just pooped out. But I wonder if that living funeral did him in."

"Maybe he just needed to say his good-byes," I said. "Once he did, he was free to pass over to the next world." I silently wished I'd had the idea for living funerals a year earlier. That way I could've exchanged a few good-byes of my own.

Aunt Josie blew her nose noisily. "Aubrey Bryant was one of the nicest men I have ever had the pleasure of knowing," she said, mopping her nose with the handkerchief. "And I'm not just saying that because he was one of mine. He was a first-class gentleman. Never took his teeth out at the table, like some of them do. Never left whiskers in the sink when he shaved. Never called me Buttercup or Sweet Dreams or anything disrespectful. I was always Miss Josie to him. And I appreciated that."

"He sure seemed to like living at your house," I contributed.

"Fourteen years he was with me," she said, nodding through her tears.

"That's a long time," I said, trying to be helpful.

We sat in silence for a moment.

"He had a vain streak," she said, now hiccuping in addition to crying. "Did you know he wore a toupee?"

"Mr. Bryant did?"

"Uh-huh," Aunt Josie confirmed. Then she giggled weakly. "He didn't tell me about it for the longest time. When it comes to hair, men can be prouder than women."

"How'd you find out about it?" I asked.

"Well, I'll tell you," she said, brightening at the memory of a good story. "His hair started looking real snarly. I told him I needed to give him a shampoo and condition before his hair turned into a rat's nest. That's when he took the toupee off his head and handed it to me, like he was handing me his hat." She laughed and then sighed heavily. "I'm sprinkling his ashes in the garden tomorrow. You want to help?"

"I can't," I said without elaborating. I knew Mother wouldn't let me, even if I wanted to. But I couldn't help asking what I'd been wondering for weeks. "What do they look like?"

"What?" asked Aunt Josie. "The ashes?"

I nodded.

"Just regular old ashes, I imagine," Aunt Josie said. "Like if you burned leaves or something."

"Did they smell like . . . burnt skin?" I asked.

"No, child," she said. Then she stopped. "Truth is, I've never actually seen anyone's ashes up close. You sure you don't want to come to the crematorium and pick 'em up with me? You can peek at the ashes as I walk Mr. Bryant home."

The whole conversation was making my mind spin like a pinwheel. "You're going to turn your back-yard into a cemetery!" I blurted.

"What are you talking about, Daralynn?"

"If you sprinkle Mr. Bryant behind your house, it'll be like having a dead *body* back there."

Aunt Josie unwrapped a stick of gum and popped it in her mouth. "Bodies underground. Ashes on the ground. What's it matter, really? It's not them. It's not where they are."

"It's not?" I asked.

"'Course not," she said, smacking her gum.

"Then where are—" I started to ask. But Aunt Josie was standing up and adjusting her bosom.

"I knew I should've ordered this jacket in a size fourteen," she said. Then, turning to me, she added in an almost shy voice: "Meet me at the crematorium tomorrow morning at ten?"

How could I say no?

SEVENTEEN

Dead Man Walking

I HAD TO FIB TO MOTHER the next morning at breakfast.

"I don't have any customers today, so I'm going to the library," I said.

It was Saturday. Mother was jabbing at the metal jaws of the toaster like they were her mortal enemies. Since she'd discontinued our subscription to *The Digginsville Daily Quill*, Mother had little to do in the morning but drink coffee and be mad at the world.

"This stupid thing has *never* worked right," she said, pulling out a charred piece of toast and throwing it in the garbage.

Nearly nine months after the crash, Mother was still mad. I guessed she'd always be that way. Saturday mornings were especially bad because her first appointment wasn't till eleven o'clock.

I looked at the clock on the stove. It was five minutes before ten. I'd have to run like the wind to get to the crematorium in time to meet Aunt Josie.

"I'm going to the library," I repeated.

"Heard you the first time," Mother said. "Come to the beauty parlor when you're done."

I left her sitting in the kitchen with a broken toaster. Anybody else in Digginsville would be dialing in to "Swap Line" to try to trade that toaster for something else. But not Mother. She didn't even turn on the radio anymore.

When I got to the crematorium, Clem was in front of the trailer, watering the geraniums with a garden hose.

"Beautiful day to be alive, isn't it?" he said, redirecting the water in the opposite direction to avoid getting me wet.

"Yessir," I said. I was out of breath from running.

"Something tells me you came by foot," he said, smiling.

"Yessir, I did."

I stepped into the shadow of the awning-covered doorway. If Mother happened to drive by and see me talking to Clem Monroe, I'd be the next corpse in town.

"I'm happy to tell you that your walking days are almost over," Clem said proudly. "A six-passenger de-luxe carriage will arrive in Digginsville two weeks from today."

"Really?"

"Would I lie to a kid who walks a mile each way to go fishing?" he asked. "I've got a pair of Clydes-dales coming, too."

"I've seen pictures of those. They're the horses with the shaggy legs, right?"

He nodded, still smiling. *Was it possible he was as nice as he seemed?* He sure was keen on this idea of a horse and carriage.

"I could've had a carriage delivered this week," he said, now watering the scraggly grass next to the trailer. "But I insisted on safety belts, which they don't normally install. It added three hundred dollars to the price, but I don't care. We don't want anyone to get hurt."

I was only half listening. My mind was too busy drawing a picture of a pair of Clydesdale horses clomping down Highway E on a snowy afternoon. It'd look just like a postcard—or a picture on a calendar. And in the fall we could use the horse and carriage for hayrack rides. Maybe Aunt Josie and Mr. Clem could use it on their wedding day. They could decorate the carriage with flowers and satin bows.

Something inside the crematorium began humming loudly. A shiver ran down my spine. I must've made a face because Mr. Clem smiled.

"Just the air conditioner," he said.

"Oh," I replied. "I thought maybe it was the . . . you know."

"The cremation chamber?" he asked gently. "It's okay. I know it's a sensitive subject."

I nodded.

"Would you like to know why I got in this line of work?" he asked.

"No sir," I said quickly. "That's your personal business."

As soon as I said it, I remembered that I was supposed to be conducting an investigation. I took a deep breath and tried again.

"I mean," I said as casually as I could, "unless you feel like telling me."

"You're a very respectful young lady," he answered. "And I *would* like to tell you. I think you're one of the few people in this town who might understand."

He turned off the water and stretched out the green hose long to drain it. Then he began to slowly coil the empty hose around his arm. When he spoke again, it was in a deeper, more somber tone.

"My uncle Seneca was a cattle rancher," Clem said. "He owned eight hundred fenced acres in Montana. I visited him every summer when I was young. He taught me to ride a horse and rope a calf."

"Bet that was fun," I said, wondering where this story was heading.

"It was," Clem recalled. "Until Uncle Seneca got older and grew suspicious of the ranchers who lived around him. He was convinced people were jealous of his success. He accused one neighbor of stealing his cattle. Another time he sued a man for feeding ground glass to his registered bulls."

"Was he?"

"No," said Clem, still winding the hose around his arm. "But Uncle Seneca didn't believe it. So every day he rode his favorite horse around the perimeter of his property, looking for trespassers. One day the horse spooked and threw Uncle Seneca. He landed on the fence."

"Good gosh, that had to hurt!" I said, trying not to snicker. I wondered if maybe the horse threw

Seneca on purpose. Probably sick of running the old coot around so he could snoop on his neighbors.

Clem looked at me with cold eyes. "Uncle Seneca was decapitated by a barbed-wire fence."

I didn't know what to say. I'd stopped breathing.

"The sheriff found Uncle Seneca's severed head on the neighbor's side of the fence," Clem stated. "There was some talk of the neighbor suing Uncle Seneca's estate for trespassing. But in the end, it all blew over."

"Did they . . . glue the head back on his body?"

"No," said Clem. "The funeral home simply dressed Uncle Seneca in his best suit and laid the body out in a coffin with his head where it should've been. They wrapped a bandanna around the neck area."

Clem walked around to the back of the trailer. He carried the coiled hose away from his body, like he was handling a king cobra. I followed him.

"But could you *see*?" I asked. "Could you tell your uncle's head wasn't connected to his body?"

"Yes," Clem replied matter-of-factly. "And that's an image that has never left me."

He dropped the hose in the grass. It landed with a heavy, dead sound. Then he took a deep breath. I remembered to breathe, too.

"You can't unsee something you've seen," Clem said, looking up to the sky like he was searching for something there. "Uncle Seneca's funeral has haunted me my entire adult life. I didn't want other people, especially children, to suffer like I have with unwanted images crowding their minds. Can you understand that?"

"Yeah," I said in a whisper.

I thought of how my brother, sister, and Daddy had looked like dolls dipped in wax at their funeral. I'd never forget that. The image was burned in my mind. The memory of them dead was starting to crowd out the memory of them alive.

"Seeing a loved one's ashes can be difficult, too," Clem said with a sad smile. "But there's a difference. There's no head or face. It's the face that haunts you."

"I know," I said.

I realized then that's why I'd never liked dolls. Their dead faces creeped me out. So why did people think giving me dead dolls would make me feel better about my dead family? It didn't make sense. All the strange things people did and said when other people died: None of it made sense.

"You won't tell anyone what I've told you, will you?" he asked. He was staring me straight in the eye.

"No sir," I murmured, almost hypnotized by this man and his stories.

"Good girl," he said. "Then I won't tell your mother how you like to watch people from your bedroom window in the middle of the night. I'm not sure she'd approve."

I almost jumped out of my skin. So he *had* seen me that night. He *did* have secrets.

I knew it.

Clem turned and walked to the front of the trailer. I walked around the other side, wondering where the heck Aunt Josie was. Then I spotted her in the distance, making her way toward the crematorium in high heels, her hips swinging with every step.

"Sorry I'm late, dears," she said when she arrived. She kissed Clem on the cheek and squeezed my hand. "We had a bad morning at the house."

"Nothing serious, I hope," Clem said, frowning.

"I made the mistake of telling the boys I was leaving town," Aunt Josie explained.

"Leaving?" I asked. "What do you mean *leaving?*"

"Oh, Daralynn," Aunt Josie said. "I haven't made it official yet, so mum's the word. But I'm—or I should say *we're*—moving to Chicago."

Clem put his arm around Aunt Josie's waist. "The

city of fat cats isn't going to know what to make of this tiger," he said.

Aunt Josie smiled, but her face looked weary. Makeup had settled in her worry lines. Her eyes were glistening with recent tears.

"You can't *move*," I said. "You can't leave Digginsville."

"Oh honey, I won't be gone all the time. Just a couple weeks every month. Right, sweetie pie?"

"That's right," Clem said. "We'll be back here plenty." He squeezed Aunt Josie's shoulders with his meaty hands.

"I've still gotta find someone to take care of my gentlemen when I'm gone," Aunt Josie said, almost like she was talking to herself. "This is all coming so soon after Mr. Bryant's passing. It's hard on my boys."

"I just hope they haven't changed their minds," Clem said. "Prepaid arrangements can bring peace of mind."

"Oh no," Aunt Josie said, using her pinkie finger to wipe a tear from the corner of her eye. "They've all agreed to buy the plans you offered them. In fact..." She opened her purse and withdrew a bulging envelope. "Here's everyone's money, payment in full. I'm buying a plan, too."

She handed the envelope to Clem.

"I'm just glad I could offer such an economical package," Clem said, sliding the envelope in his shirt pocket. "Now then, let me retrieve Mr. Bryant's ashes so you can gently reposition his earthly remains."

"That's such a lovely way of putting it, dear," said Aunt Josie. She smiled and put on her pretty face.

Clem held the trailer door open for Aunt Josie and me. He disappeared into a side room while Aunt Josie and I stayed in the reception area. It was dark, like the funeral home, but much smaller. Banners from Mr. Bryant's living funeral (LONG LIVE AUBREY BRYANT!) still decorated the walls.

I couldn't believe I was standing there in a crematorium—*a crematorium!*—next to Aunt Josie, who was moving away. *Leaving me!* I knew I should've felt mad or sad, but I couldn't. None of it felt real. I didn't feel anything except for that floaty feeling I'd had on the day of the funeral. This time I was floating above Aunt Josie and me, watching myself look at Aunt Josie as she sniffled and fixed her makeup.

Minutes later, Clem returned with two small black plastic bags. He handed them to Aunt Josie, who began to whimper.

"There's nothing more natural than returning a

body to the earth," Clem said softly. "No chemicals in the body. None in the earth. Just the circle of life in its purest form."

Aunt Josie nodded while continuing to sob gently.

"A windy day is best," Clem instructed. "Let the ashes fly and be free."

Aunt Josie and I left to walk Mr. Aubrey Bryant the six blocks back to our street.

"Do you mind if we take the alley?" I asked. On top of everything else, I was worried about a possible run-in with Mother.

"Fine by me, child," Aunt Josie said. "I want your mama to see us even less than you do."

EiGHTEEN

Catch of the Day

WHEN WE RETURNED TO AUNT JOSIE'S HOUSE, the four remaining tenants of The Summer Sunset Retirement Home for Distinguished Gentlemen were sitting on the front porch. Wrinkled, silent, and motionless, they looked like lizards.

"If you boys want to help Daralynn and me scatter Mr. Aubrey Bryant's ashes, please join us in the garden," Aunt Josie announced. "If you'd rather not, I understand."

None of the lizard men moved their bodies, but their gazes all dropped downward toward their laps. I didn't know if they were sad on account of Mr. Bryant's passing or because Aunt Josie was going to Chicago. Probably both.

"That's fine, darlings," Aunt Josie hollered up to the lizard men on the porch. "Just sit there and be comfortable. Daralynn and I'll take care of this other matter."

The two of us walked along the side of the house to the backyard. The July heat had already ravaged her petunias. Other blooms were hanging by a thread.

"I've never done this before," Aunt Josie whispered, slowly opening the first bag of ashes. "Maybe we could just sprinkle them around the hydrangeas and purple coneflowers."

She grabbed a handful of ashes and flung it gently under a flowering bush. They looked like just regular old ashes from the fireplace. I couldn't fathom for the life of me how that could be Mr. Aubrey Bryant.

"What's he feel like?" I asked.

"Hard to say," Aunt Josie replied. She was closing her eyes. "I'm trying not to think about it too much. Honey, you don't have to do this if you don't want to."

"No, I want to help," I lied. I reached in the bag and pulled out a small handful. "It smells like the burnt stuff I scrape off Mother's Parker House rolls."

Aunt Josie grabbed another handful. "That's what we'll pretend it is—burnt dinner rolls," she said, sprinkling a big handful of ashes around a clump of purple coneflowers.

I extracted a second handful from the bag. This time, along with the ashes, I got tiny bone fragments. I stared at what I held in my hand.

"I know, honey," Aunt Josie said gently. "But isn't it nice to think Mr. Bryant will be part of this garden? It *does* feel natural, doesn't it? Clem said to release the ashes to the wind, but I think I'd prefer to keep him right here at home. I'll never be able to look at a flower from this garden again without thinking Mr. Aubrey Bryant's in there somewhere."

Maybe it was disrespectful to think about my own problems at the time, but I couldn't help it.

"I don't want you to go to Chicago with Mr. Clem," I said.

"Oh child," she replied. She placed the bag of ashes in the grass so she could put her arm around my shoulder. "I know this is hard on you. It's hard on me, too. But you'll come visit me in Chicago. We'll just have to talk your mother into it. I'm sure we can."

"When pigs fly," I mumbled. "I never get to go anywhere. She wants me at home or at the beauty parlor twenty-four hours a day."

"Now don't you go gettin' all sulky on me," Aunt Josie said in her fake bossy voice. "We'll be back in Digginsville every month. Mr. Clem's not giving up the crematorium. And I'm not giving up my house or business."

I nodded silently and grabbed another handful of ashes from the bag. Aunt Josie did the same.

"Did you know," said Aunt Josie, changing the subject, "the reason Mr. Clem got into the crematin' business? It was because of his uncle Seneca."

"Yeah, he told me about him," I said, conjuring up my new unwanted mental image of a decapitated corpse.

Aunt Josie started giggling. "Can you *imagine* seeing such a thing?" She whooped with laughter. "I would've paid fifty dollars to see that!"

"You *would*?" I asked. I didn't even like thinking about it.

"Oh, I shouldn't laugh," she said, covering her mouth with the back of her hand. "But the thought of a dead body falling from the bottom of a coffin just tickles me blind."

"Are you talking about the cattle rancher in Montana?"

"That's right," confirmed Aunt Josie. "His name was Seneca. He was Mr. Clem's uncle. He must've been a big old boy to bust out the bottom of a coffin." Aunt Josie snorted. "But that's exactly what happened when they were carrying him out of the church. *Blam!* Out he falls! And poor Clem just a young boy, seeing all that. 'Course he can laugh about it now. But that's the sort of thing that'd scar a child, don't you imagine? And it certainly explains how he got into the crematin' business."

"Huh?" I said. "That's not what he told me."

But Aunt Josie was too busy giggling to listen. "You can't unsee a sight like that," she rattled on, now flinging the ashes in generous handfuls. "Better not to see it in the first place. Well, I agree with him on that point, though I think I would've liked to see the old goat fall out of his coffin. He was the jealous type, Clem says. Do you know Seneca sued every one of his neighbors for making eyes at his wife? The stress of being jealous finally caused an artery to blow up in Uncle Seneca's brain. He died on the court-house square."

"Mr. Clem told me something different. He said—"

But our conversation was interrupted by a cough behind us. Aunt Josie and I turned around. The four lizard men were standing with the banner they'd carried in the Fourth of July parade.

"Oh sweethearts," Aunt Josie said, placing both hands over her heart. "That's just perfect for this occasion. Mr. Aubrey Bryant would be so pleased. Just stand right where you are in parade formation while Daralynn and I finish with the scattering." Then in a softer voice, she said to me: "Let's pick up the pace here, Daralynn. It's a hot day and I don't want any of my boys keeling over with a heatstroke."

We worked for a few more minutes, sprinkling handfuls of Mr. Aubrey Bryant around Aunt Josie's flowers. My hands were covered in the remains of the man who, just a week ago, had lived down the street from me. And now here I was, holding him in my hands. I looked behind me at the lizard men standing with their banner, their eyes still lowered, like flags flying at half-mast.

"You about ready to call it quits?" Aunt Josie asked quietly.

"Uh-huh," I said.

"All rightie then," Aunt Josie said in voice loud enough for the lizard men to hear. "We've got just a bit left. What do y'all think of saving a little of Mr. Aubrey Bryant's remains in a pretty glass pudding bowl? We could put him on the mantel. That way, he'd always be with us."

The men nodded in unison. So we marched as a group with the remaining ashes back to the house.

"You're welcome to stay for lunch," Aunt Josie told me.

But I'd lost my appetite for food. "No thanks. I'm going out to Doc Lake for a little while."

And that's what I did.

My head felt like a popcorn kettle exploding with worries as I walked the well-worn path along Highway E toward the lake. So dang much was happening and none of it was good. I needed time to think it all through. All I had were questions and problems without any answers or solutions.

When I got to the lake, I saw Sonny and Joyce McMurtrey fishing on the other side. I waved in their direction, hoping they'd stay where they were. Luckily, they did. I needed time and space to think.

I sat in the grass for a while and stared at the water. Then I picked up a stick and started poking at the scum on the lake. I was trying to think how I'd explain this day in a letter to Daddy, Wayne Junior, and Lilac Rose. But for some reason, my mind circled back to Bud Mosley and his broken aquarium. I wondered if he ever found anyone to swap for that. Then I wondered how it got cracked in the first place. Maybe his cat, Pickles, was trying to catch a fish in the aquarium and knocked it over.

I was poking at the lake scum for an hour or more. A nest of some kind had blown in the lake and was floating on the water. Without thinking, I maneuvered my stick under the nest and dragged the wet clump over to the side of the lake.

When I did, I saw it wasn't a nest at all. It was a mat of gray fur. I pulled it out of the water using two sticks like salad tongs. I tried to dry the dripping tangle of fur by shaking it. I was trying to guess what kind of animal it had come from. It was too light for a muskrat. Maybe a possum, I thought.

I moved behind a sticker bush so Sonny and Joyce wouldn't see me playing with a dead pelt. I kept shaking it with a stick so I could see what the fur looked like dry. That's when I realized it wasn't fur. It was a little gray wig the size of *Le Frenchie.*

I was still studying it when I heard a car horn honk. I turned around and saw Mother, pulling into the parking lot near the cookout grills. She was getting out of the car. She held something small in her hand.

I hid the hairpiece under a sticker bush and walked toward her. Even from a distance I could see what she was holding: my library card.

"Get in the car," she yelled. "You're grounded."

NiNETEEN

A Burning Mystery

BOY, DID I GET AN EARFUL on the drive home.

"I have never been so angry in my life," Mother began.

"I just—" I said, trying to explain.

"I am *talking!*" she hissed. "When I got to the beauty parlor this morning and saw your library card stuck in a corner of your mirror, I decided to walk it over to the library. I thought you'd need it to check out books. But Mrs. Jan Whitehead told me you hadn't been in today. And then her assistant, Miss Carrie Cline, said she'd seen you standing in front of the crematorium earlier this morning, talking to Mr. Clem and Aunt Josie."

Mother took a deep breath as if to steady herself. She was mad enough to burst into flames.

"I was only there because—" I put in quickly.

"If you want to associate with those two *operators*," she interrupted, "you can just be my guest. Just *be* my guest. I have enough on my plate trying to take care of Mamaw and my customers and the house and the yard. I swear, you can just *live* with Aunt Josie, if that's what you want. Just go down there and *live* with her."

"She's moving to Chicago with—"

"I don't want to *hear* it!" Mother yelled. The tires were screeching as we turned in our driveway. She got out on her side and slammed the car door with all her strength. Then she walked up the porch steps.

"I had some thinking to do," I said, unfolding myself from my side of the car. "And I like to do my thinking at Doc Lake, just like Daddy used to do."

She stopped on the porch, turned, and looked me dead in the eyes. "You did *not* have my permission to go to the lake."

My stomach turned sour at the sound of those familiar words. This was the same reason I'd been grounded last October. It was the reason I wasn't in Daddy's plane when it crashed.

"I was only trying to . . ." I stopped. There was no

sense explaining myself, so I switched gears. "I'm too *old* to be grounded."

"Oh, is that so?" Mother said. "You're too *old* to be grounded. That's news to me. Go to your room. *Now.* You're grounded for the rest of the summer."

"Fine!" I cried. "Why don't you just ground me for the rest of my *life?*"

"Good idea. You're grounded for the rest of your *life.*"

"SEE IF I CARE!" I yelled as I ran upstairs. I tripped over a pile of dolls on the landing. "I hate these damn things! They're stupid and *dead!* Everything in this house is dead! I bet you wish *I* were dead, too, don't you? DON'T YOU?"

I slammed my bedroom door as hard as I could. Then I stood in my room and waited, my hands braced against the door like I was a human blockade. In my mind I dared my mother to try to punish me for cursing.

Just try it! I dare you! But she didn't come upstairs.

Minutes later, I heard Mother on the phone in the front hallway. It was obvious who she'd called.

"Yes, in fact I *do* mind," Mother was saying. I put my head against my bedroom door. The attic fan was drowning out most of what she was saying. I could hear only bits and pieces: "What people think" and "You wouldn't know because you don't *have* any children, Josie" and "An absolute disgrace to the family."

I couldn't tell if Mother was talking about me or Aunt Josie. Either way, it made me furious. I abandoned my position at the door and flopped on my bed in a rage.

Two hours later, I heard Mother knock on my door and set something in the hallway. I could tell from the smell what it was: a Salisbury steak TV dinner and a burnt Parker House roll.

Like I wanted to eat *that*!

I didn't want dinner. I wanted to know why Mr. Clem was telling different stories to Aunt Josie and me. I wanted to know why he was so keen on his horse-and-carriage idea when he had the nicest car in town. I wanted to know why he'd stolen my idea for living funerals, and what he'd meant when he said it was a beautiful day to be alive. Was there a beautiful day to be *dead*?

More than anything else, I wanted to know if he was so nice and generous, why did he remind me of a big, mean snake stuck in a small, cracked aquarium?

But now I was grounded. I couldn't do any investigating. I couldn't do anything.

I reached under my bed and pulled out my book of *Pertinent Facts & Important Information*. I started writing:

Dear Daddy, Wayne Junior, and Lilac Rose,

This has been a flat-out rotten day from beginning to end.

I stopped. I was too restless to write.

Instead, I stared at myself in the mirror. My hair was starting to grow out. I mussed it up with my hands and squinted at my reflection. I looked like Wayne Junior, after he got back from sleepaway camp.

When I got tired of looking at myself, I looked at the reflection of my room in the mirror. I stared at the chair in the corner where Daddy had taught me how to read a flight schedule so I'd know where his postcards were coming from. I looked at my messy bed, where Lilac Rose had crawled in with me a million times when she woke up from a nightmare and couldn't fall back to sleep. I used to do the same thing with Wayne Junior when I was little and scared.

They were all dead. Gone. There was nothing I could do about it.

And now Aunt Josie was leaving me. She wasn't dying, but she was moving to Chicago, which from my point of view was as bad as dying. Worse yet, she was going with a man I had a bad feeling about.

My head hurt from thinking about it. But if I didn't think harder, something terrible might happen.

I crawled in bed and closed my eyes. I pulled the covers over my head, defeated by my investigation. But it was no good. There was no chance of sleeping at seven o'clock on a summer night. I flipped and flopped for an hour like a fish out of water.

Fishing. It was the only thing I wanted to do right then. Daddy always said the brain works best when you stop thinking and start fishing. So that's what I did.

Standing on my bed with an imaginary pole in my hand, I cast off into an invisible body of water in my room. I reeled in and cast off again, dozens of times. Then I began fly-fishing with my other hand, rocking my invisible line back and forth from ten to two, ten to two. I was reeling in speckled trout with one pole and bluegill and catfish with the other.

I fished with flair and acrobatics. I jumped from

my bed to Lilac Rose's, dodging giant white sharks that were trying to kill me. I didn't think about anything but fishing.

I pretended I was Pickles, fishing for dinner in Bud Mosley's aquarium. Then I pretended I was me, deep-sea fishing with Clem in Key West.

I caught a mackerel. Holy mackerel! Then an octopus. I jumped from bed to bed, flying and fishing! I thought I saw a jellyfish.

And then Uncle Seneca's head floated by.

It was only a doll's head that rolled out from under Lilac Rose's bed. But it stopped me cold. My hands fell to my sides. My imaginary fishing poles disappeared. I stood on my bed like a bird on a tree bough. The idea of seeing Uncle Seneca's head in the water paralyzed me.

With that image in my mind everything made sense, including the dinner that was waiting for me in the hallway.

I opened my bedroom door. The Salisbury steak TV dinner was cold and congealed. It didn't interest me as a meal or as a clue. But the Parker House roll was different. It contained a secret I could feel in my bones.

I stared at the cold burnt roll, my heart still beating fast from my fishing expedition. Slowly, I picked up the roll and held it to my nose, inhaling deeply.

I *knew* it.

I waited until midnight, when I knew Mother would be asleep. Then I dressed silently, barely breathing. I grabbed my book of *Pertinent Facts & Important Information* and crept downstairs.

In the basement I found Daddy's tackle box where I'd left it two Sundays before. I used a flashlight to find the tooth I'd fished out of the lake. I stuck the tooth in my front pocket. Then I dug out the biggest, heaviest trawling hook I could find, and stuck it through my belt loop. I slid a couple of line sinkers in my back pocket, along with the flashlight. Finally, I grabbed my fishing pole and tiptoed back upstairs to the den, where I'd left my book.

With all my gear in tow, I walked as quietly as I could through the breezeway into Mamaw's house. I left through her back door. I couldn't risk waking up Mother with our squeaky screen door.

TWENTY

Go Fish

The night was black with a little toenail clipping of a moon hanging all alone in the sky. It looked like how I felt.

I walked fast. The familiar path I'd hiked so many times by day felt different at this hour. I kept seeing things that weren't there: snakes, dolls, decapitated heads. I suspected what I might find in Doc Lake, but I wasn't sure. I hated to think something so bad could happen in Digginsville.

When I finally got to the lake, I found the spot where I'd been the previous day. I put my book down at my feet and turned on the flashlight so I could hook the trawler on my fishing line. But the second I turned on the light, I saw something under a tree.

"What brings you out here on a nice summer night?" Mr. Clem yelled. He was maybe forty yards away.

I stopped breathing. "Nothin'," I hollered back in a high voice. "Nothin' at all, sir."

My eyes scanned the lake. I spotted his yellow car parked on the opposite side of the water. No other vehicles were in sight. No other people. Just me and Mr. Clem.

He started walking toward me along the water's edge. "You don't even have your tackle box with you," he said with a laugh.

"No sir," I said, watching him get closer to me. I felt dizzy with fear.

"Is that a book you've brought to read?" he asked, eyeballing my book of *Pertinent Facts & Important Information.* "Or is that your diary?"

"No," I said. "It's just . . . a book."

I tried to float above myself. I tried to rise up and out of my body, like I'd done before. I wanted to hover over myself, to not be there, to just observe it all from a safe distance.

But I couldn't do it. My body felt heavy and stiff, like a statue. Like a gravestone. Like a corpse.

"You can't very well read by moonlight," Clem

said. He was taking slow, deliberate steps in my direction. "I bet I know why you're here on a hot night. You're planning to do a little swimming, aren't you?"

"I'm not here to swim," I said, backing up slowly.

"Oh, I bet you are," he said. "Even though I *told* you how dangerous swimming without a lifeguard can be."

"I'm not here to swim," I said again.

"Now, now," he said with a hollow laugh. "I know all about you and your misbehaving. You seem to have a hard time minding adults, don't you, Dolly?"

"No."

"That's not what I've heard," he replied. "After all your mother's been through, you're still disobeying her."

He knows too much about me. He knows exactly where to strike.

He was getting closer. From the back of Mrs. Staniss's class to the chalkboard—that's how close he was.

"But do you know what I think?" he asked. "I think this is a perfect night to break the rules. I think this is the night you and I should go for a swim."

"I don't want to," I whispered.

"What did you say?" he asked. "I can't hear you."

"I don't *want* to."

Move faster. Just get the toupee and get out of here.

"Don't be silly," Clem said. "I won't tell anyone. Let's go swimming."

He was ten feet away. I could see his face clearly. The moonlight reflected off his shiny white teeth. I pointed my fishing pole directly at him like a sword. He just laughed.

"You wouldn't hit me with that thing, would you?" he asked. His voice was mocking, but I didn't care. I knew exactly why he was there. I knew what was in that lake. Or rather, *who* was in the lake. I was the only person in Digginsville who had figured out Clem's secret. And he knew I knew.

I shined my flashlight at Clem's eyes while I looked in the dark for the sticker bush. I kept my fishing pole aimed at him like a weapon.

"You'd have to insert that pole directly into my eye socket to do any real harm," he said. "Is your aim that good, Dolly? Is it?"

I was pretty sure I knew which bush it was under. I'd have only one chance to get it. Quickly, with one smooth motion, I pivoted my body and stuck my fishing pole under the bush. I dragged the matted hairpiece out, all the while shining the flashlight in Clem's eyes.

When I had the toupee in my hand, I threw the fishing pole at Clem as hard as I could. I threw my flashlight at him, too. It hit him in the face.

"Hey!" he yelled. "That hurt. Now wait just a minute!"

But I didn't wait. I grabbed my *Pertinent Facts & Important Information* book and Mr. Aubrey Bryant's toupee and started running.

I cut through the woods. My heart felt like fireworks going off inside my body. Within minutes, I could hear the low sound of Clem's convertible slithering down Highway E. Where the trees were thin, I could even see his headlights. They were like big yellow snake eyes, looking for me.

I ran through the scratchy woods, hoping my instincts were right. I knew if I started second-guessing myself, I'd get turned around and never find my way out. I pretended I was a pilot, flying on a secret night mission. I tried to fool myself into thinking I wasn't scared to death.

When the woods ended and town started, I took the alley. Avis Brown's white Oldsmobile was parked in her driveway. I knocked on her back door. No answer.

I knocked again, harder. And then again. My

frantic heartbeat was keeping time with the sounds of big-winged night insects hovering around me. I started pounding on the door.

When Avis finally answered, it was obvious by her curlers that I'd awakened the publisher of *The Digginsville Daily Quill.*

"Dolly," she said. "What's wrong? Where's your mother?"

"Mother's fine," I said. "The reason I'm here is this." I showed her Aubrey Bryant's toupee.

"If that's a dead animal you've found, it can wait until morning," she said, rubbing her eyes.

I told her it wasn't a dead animal, and that it couldn't wait one minute more. So she invited me in and made a pot of coffee. Sitting at her kitchen table, I told Avis Brown everything I knew. I used my book of *Pertinent Facts & Important Information* for exact dates and quotes.

"Unbelievable," Avis said, paging through my book. "Simply unbelievable."

"Don't pay any attention to the Dear Daddys and all that stuff," I said. It occurred to me only then that maybe I should be embarrassed for writing all those letters to my deceased family members.

But Avis didn't seem to think that part was strange at all. She threw a housecoat over her nightgown and drove us like a bullet to Sheriff Walter Whipple's house.

I felt bad for waking up the sheriff and his wife. But they said it was okay.

"Comes with the job," Sheriff Whipple said. Then he turned to Avis. "You want to tell me what's gonna be on the front page of your next edition?"

"I'd rather let Dolly tell you," Avis said.

So I did, right there in the Whipples' kitchen. Sheriff Whipple listened carefully while studying the tooth and the toupee. He even thumbed through my book. He was still wearing his plaid pajamas when he started making phone calls.

Jimmy Chuck Walters arrived just as Mrs. Whipple was pouring pancake batter in her skillet. Avis said we'd have to take a rain check on breakfast.

By four o'clock in the morning, I was back at Doc Lake, watching men in canoes glide silently across the silver water. The search crew, led by Uncle Waldo, included members of the Digginsville Volunteer Fire Department. They dragged the lake using long poles with hooks and nets.

Less than one hour later, I saw the late Mr. Aubrey Bryant being pulled to shore. His bloated, naked, bald-headed body was harshly illuminated by a search light. Just before sunrise, a second body was found.

It was obvious what had happened and who was to blame. But by then, Clem Monroe was long gone.

TWENTY-ONE

Wanted!

I NEVER DID GO TO SLEEP that night. At eight o'clock in the morning I was in the kitchen when Mother came down to make coffee. I tried to tell her the grim news, but after two or three sentences she rushed back up to her bedroom and got dressed. Then she ran outside and stole Uncle Waldo's copy of *The Digginsville Daily Quill* from his porch steps. The story was on the front page.

Two Bodies Found in Doc Lake;
Warrant Issued for Clem Monroe's Arrest

by Avis Brown

Two dead bodies were discovered early Sunday morning in Doc Lake.

The first body, that of Aubrey Bryant, age 89, was found shortly before five A.M. The second body was found not long after that.

Some of us suspect the second body belongs to the California lady who died on Highway 60 a while back. But Sheriff Whipple isn't saying yes or no. He has to get dental records to make sure.

If you've been reading your *Daily Quill* lately, you know that Mr. Bryant died of a heart attack last Monday. He was supposedly cremated shortly thereafter at Clem's Crematorium.

Ms. Gail Rowland (the California lady) died in a terrible car accident almost three weeks ago. Her family asked that she be cremated at Clem's Crematorium rather than shipping the body back to California.

Well, it's crystal clear, to this reporter anyway, that at least one and possibly two cremations never took place, judging from what authorities found in Doc Lake.

And it just gets worse from there.

When authorities went to the Crossroads Hotel at approximately six o'clock this morning to question Mr. Clem Monroe, they discovered that he and his Cadillac were gone, as were all of his clothes.

(I'm told Mr. Monroe hadn't paid his hotel bill, either.)

A warrant has been issued for the arrest of Clem Monroe.

His local lady friend, Joanne Cecilia "Josie" Oakland, is being questioned by police even as I type these words.

A reliable source in the case who asked to remain anonymous tells me that ashes in a pudding bowl on Josie's mantel are purportedly the remains of Mr. Aubrey Bryant. But we'll see about that, won't we?

The pudding bowl and ashes are on their way to the Missouri Crime Lab in Jefferson City for analysis.

Mother read the story twice before picking up the phone.

"Avis? It's Hattie," Mother began. She was pacing back and forth across the kitchen floor, as far as the cord would reach. "What about the horse and carriage?"

I had completely forgotten about that. I guessed Avis had, too.

"How many people did he swindle for that boondoggle?" Mother asked, talking fast. "I bet you a *lot* of people, but they won't like admitting it now. Someone's going to have to get sworn affidavits from everyone in town. And what about that California family? Did he send them anything in the mail? If so, that's interstate commerce and the FBI should be all over this thing."

All those *Perry Mason* episodes were finally paying off.

Mother paused to listen to Avis Brown. She nodded at the phone. "I understand," she said. "Right. Good point. I agree with you there, Avis, one hundred percent."

Then Mother was looking at me with a funny expression on her face. "No, I didn't realize that. Oh, really? Well, yes, now that you mention it, she was saying something about that this morning when she . . . She did *what?*"

Now Mother was glaring at me. I squirmed in my chair.

"Is that a fact?" Mother said slowly. "Well, I appreciate all *your* hard work, too, Avis. Good-bye."

She hung up the phone and crossed her arms.

"I *had* to," I said. "I was worried about Aunt Josie. She was going to move to Chicago with him. And now . . . now she could be going to *jail.*"

"Aunt Josie's not going to jail," Mother said matter-of-factly. "This wasn't her fault."

But all of Aunt Josie's gentlemen had purchased prepaid cremation plans, which they wouldn't have done without her nudging them along. It was their money in the bulging envelope, along with Aunt Josie's and the donations for the horse and carriage, that Clem Monroe took with him when he left Digginsville.

I was too busy worrying about the money to realize that in addition to everything else he took, Clem Monroe had also stolen Aunt Josie's heart.

TWENTY-TWO

Gone and Never Coming Back

MOTHER SKIPPED CHURCH THAT SUNDAY so she could devote herself fully to the breaking news.

After returning Uncle Waldo's newspaper to his porch, she took a broom out to our porch and began sweeping the front steps. Then she started whistling. For once, she was clearly hoping Uncle Waldo would come out of his house to talk. But Uncle Waldo's house was quiet. Mother eventually gave up and went inside.

"Keep your eye on Mamaw," Mother ordered me over her shoulder. My grandmother had almost a hundred dolls lined up in military formation on our front porch. In all the excitement, I'd forgotten to hide them from her the night before.

It wasn't until after lunch that I saw Uncle Waldo walking down the sidewalk from the direction of Aunt Josie's house.

"Hello, Baby man!" Mamaw hollered his way. "Want to play dolls?"

Uncle Waldo smiled weakly. "Maybe another time."

Mother must've heard him from inside the house because she ran out to the porch. "Waldo!" she said with an exuberant wave of her arm. "Is Josie all right?"

"She will be," Uncle Waldo replied in a tired voice. "She's been down at the police station all morning, answering questions. They finally released her a little while ago."

"Thank heavens," Mother said.

I couldn't tell if she was being sincere or not.

"Sheriff Whipple said her only crime was falling in love with a flimflam man," Uncle Waldo said, rubbing his temples. "I tried to tell her to slow it down with that guy. But you know Josie."

"Oh yes," Mother said, nodding. "I certainly do."

"I know Josie, too," Mamaw chimed in. "She's real pretty."

Uncle Waldo laughed. "She *is* pretty, isn't she? Now if you'll excuse me, ladies, I'm ready for a nap."

"Of course," Mother said in her best company voice.

Uncle Waldo turned toward his house, but stopped when his eyes met mine. "Excellent work," he said.

"Thanks," I mumbled. I scratched my chigger bites, trying not to make eye contact with Mother.

Late that afternoon, a thunderstorm moved through town, cooling things down and providing the dramatic soundtrack the day called for. I sat on the porch swing, listening to the rain hammer down on our house. I thought about what had transpired.

For almost a whole month, a common criminal had lived among us. It was going to take a while for that to sink in.

And Digginsville wasn't going to get a horse and carriage.

And Aunt Josie wasn't moving to Chicago. At least that part was good. But then I felt guilty for feeling glad about that.

Poor Aunt Josie. As the summer storm lumbered past Digginsville, the sound of thunder was replaced by the sound of crying coming from her porch. Her sobs hung in the moist air like wet laundry on a clothesline.

Uncle Waldo must've heard her, too, because he came out of his house and sat on a porch chair. Mother, Mamaw, and I were all sitting on our porch. I was pretending to read an old *National Geographic.* Mother was brushing out fake hair extensions. Mamaw was rocking her dolls, one by one.

"I . . . Oh! . . . The *nerve* of that man!" Aunt Josie cried from her porch.

Uncle Waldo sighed loudly.

"I never thought . . . I just never *ever* thought," Aunt Josie wailed.

Uncle Waldo stood up. "I better go back down there," he said from across the yard.

"No," Mother said, stuffing the hair weaves back in the plastic bag. "You stay. I'll go. Daralynn, you stay here."

She marched down the porch steps and turned left, toward Aunt Josie's house.

At first the sobs became softer until they disappeared all together. I could just picture Mother standing with her arms crossed in front of Aunt Josie, telling her what a darn fool she'd been to trust Mr. Clem in the first place.

Then, sure enough, ten minutes later the crying

was worse than ever. It sounded like someone was dying.

I jumped off the porch and ran down the sidewalk. Good gosh! Aunt Josie didn't need Mother to point out all the dang mistakes she'd made. She needed someone who could make her feel better, not worse.

As I sprinted toward the end of the block, the cries from Aunt Josie's porch were getting louder, more desperate sounding. Almost bloodcurdling.

"He's gone, and he's never coming back! He's gone, and he's *never* coming back!"

I ran faster, feeling madder at Mother with every cry. When I got to Aunt Josie's house, I took the porch steps two by two. I was almost to the very top before I stopped. What I saw could've knocked me over with a feather.

It wasn't Aunt Josie crying after all. It was Mother. Her head was in Aunt Josie's lap.

"He's gone, and he's never coming back," Mother sobbed.

"I know," Aunt Josie said, petting Mother's hair. "Let it out, Hattie. Just let it all out."

I backed away quietly. I knew Mother wouldn't

want me to see her like that. So I walked home and listened from our porch as Mother and Aunt Josie cried together most of the night. They were two women in love with men who were long gone and never coming back.

TWENTY-THREE

Mother's Funeral

THE NEXT DAY WE STARTED PLANNING Mother's living funeral. She invited everyone in town. We held it the following Saturday afternoon at Danielson Family Funeral Home.

Mother wore the same navy blue suit she'd worn to the funeral for Daddy, Lilac Rose, and Wayne Junior. The jacket and skirt hung more loosely on her because of all the weight she'd lost. She wore her hair pulled back in her signature black bun.

I wore the same dumb dress I'd worn before. It was tighter on me and quite a bit shorter on account of how much I'd grown over the past nine months. Mother slicked down my hair with a generous glob of Dippity-Do. I tried to be agreeable because I knew this was important to her. At least she didn't make me wear gloves.

We used a glossy display casket as a buffet table, just like we did at Uncle Waldo's living funeral. Our sandwich selection included cucumber and cream cheese, tomato and mayonnaise, and pimento cheese. Mamaw helped for a while, but then retreated to a corner with her dolls for most of the afternoon.

We played fake classical music on the stereo until it was time for the eulogy, which Mother delivered herself.

"I want to thank you all for coming today," she began. "I'm glad to see everyone's doing well in spite of what we've been through lately, which hasn't been entirely pleasant."

"You got that right," someone in the crowd said. Heads nodded in agreement.

"I'd like to give that Mr. Clem a piece of my mind," someone else said.

"I can certainly appreciate that," Mother said. "But I wanted to talk about something else today, if you don't mind." She cleared her throat nervously. "As you know, I lost my husband, my son, and my baby girl in a plane crash last October. And I'm ashamed to admit this, but . . . well, for a long time, I wished I'd died in that crash, too."

I knew it.

"But that was crazy thinking on my part," she continued, her voice quivering. "Because I have so much to live for. Just look around this room. Look at all these wonderful friends I have, all this support I've had. All the casseroles and pies you brought to my home last fall. I don't think I even remembered to thank you all for that. So I want to say thank you now."

"You're welcome, Hattie," someone in the back said.

"It's no trouble to make a pie," another voice added.

"It certainly has been for me lately," Mother said. She was trying to laugh but her voice got caught on a tear. "I want to thank my family, too. I have a brother-in-law who's become a neighbor. I have a sister-in-law who's become like a sister to me. I have mother who's become . . . like a daughter."

Everyone was looking at Mamaw, who was in the back of the room, tearing off pieces of a tomato sandwich and feeding them to her dolls. She waved to the crowd. I hadn't thought about it like that before, but

Mamaw *had* become sort of like Lilac Rose—or what Lilac Rose was like when she was four or five years old.

"And I have a daughter," Mother said, looking directly at me, "who's . . . who's been a lifesaver for me."

A line of tears was rolling down her cheek now. Mother had done so little emoting in her life. Listening to her now was like listening to me when I first learned to read. There was no stopping her.

"I'm sure you all know," Mother added softly, "that Daralynn was her daddy's favorite."

What? Was this true? Good gosh, nobody ever tells me anything!

But there it was, just like that: a postcard from Daddy. For me. I should've known it'd take this long to arrive. (Did I mention how slow mail delivery was in Digginsville?)

I smiled a big happy-cat smile at all the people staring at me, which was every single person in that funeral home. I could've cried, too, right then and there. But I closed my throat tight to keep the tears down.

Mother was still talking. "And I thank the good Lord that Daralynn disobeys from time to time.

Otherwise I'd have nobod—" Her voice broke off. She shook her head back and forth before resuming. "There's no denying my family's smaller now. But that just means we have to love each other harder."

"Does this mean I can play my music as loud as I want, and not have to worry about you *crabbing* about it?" Aunt Josie asked from the first row.

Everybody laughed.

"Yes, it does," said Mother. "In fact, I might even thank you for providing some evening entertainment now and then."

"Now don't turn all sugary sweet on us," teased Aunt Josie. "You wouldn't be yourself without a little vinegar."

Even after all the commotion, you could always count on Aunt Josie to lighten the mood when necessary.

"One more thing," Mother said. "And I don't mean this as a criticism of anyone because I know you don't mean it that way. But I wish you all would stop calling my daughter Dolly. Dolls are lifeless reproductions of little girls. After the events of this past week, I hope you'll agree with me that Daralynn is one of the most alive, most beautiful, and certainly one of the *bravest* young women this town has ever seen."

Oh, jeez. Now this was getting just downright embarrassing.

I smiled as politely as I could, but narrowed my eyes on Mother. I was trying to give her the sign to move on already. She just smiled back at me. So I smiled back with big saucer eyes that clearly said: *Mother, get on with it, please!*

"All right then," she said, "we have sandwiches and cake and ice cream. I apologize that the cake's store-bought from the Schwan's man. But I hope you'll enjoy it. Please make yourself at home. And thank you for coming."

"Wait, please."

It was Uncle Waldo. He was standing up in the third row.

"Before everyone goes, there's something I'd like to ask Hattie. And as God is my witness, I'd like to make this a public request."

TWENTY-FOUR

Uncle Waldo's Proposal

A HUSH FELL OVER THE ROOM.

"Waldo," said Mother. "I'm sure this can wait till we—"

"No, it can't wait, Hattie," Uncle Waldo declared.

He cleared his throat and turned his body so that he was facing not just Mother, but the whole room. Then he continued, almost prayerfully.

"Many of you might remember that I came back from Vietnam six years ago," he said. "Since then, I've spent most of that time living with my sister and helping out as best I could with the men who share her home. Some of you surely must've wondered why I didn't get a so-called real job after I got back. Well, I'll tell you."

Uncle Waldo paused to take a deep breath. "In the war, I did things I'm not proud of. I saw things no person should ever be witness to. They're things I'll never be able to forget. I had a full head of hair when I went to war. This is what trauma can do to a body."

Uncle Waldo lowered his head for emphasis. The room was silent. All eyes, even Mamaw's, were staring at his shiny bald head. After a moment he looked up and cleared his throat again nervously. Making speeches was no more Uncle Waldo's style than gushing about love was Mother's.

"What Hattie and Daralynn have been through is as terrible as anything that happened to me in the war," Uncle Waldo continued. "Psychologists have big names for what I'm talking about here, for what Hattie and Daralynn have been going through, and what I went through, and am still going through. But it's really not that complicated. I've come to believe that if you live on this earth long enough, you're bound to be traumatized by something or someone. Life can beat you up bad and kick you in the teeth. You might try to hide from it. That's what I did. For six years, I basically hid out in Josie's attic. It was all I could do some mornings just to get out of bed. But day by day, I got stronger."

"God bless America and our brave veterans!" cried a voice from the crowd.

"God bless Waldo!" chimed in another voice.

Uncle Waldo paused before continuing. "Some of you probably know that I recently bought the house next to Hattie and Daralynn. Living next door to them has been the most—"

"For the love of Jesus!" cried Aunt Josie, stomping her high-heeled shoe. "If you're asking Hattie to marry you, just come out and—"

"Josie!" interrupted Mother. "That's not what he's saying!"

"Well, it's what he *should* be saying," Aunt Josie countered.

"Ladies, please," Uncle Waldo said firmly. "What I'm trying to say is that life is hard—for everybody. None of us gets out of here without getting our hearts broken in one way or another. You can try to make sense of it. You can try to find reasons and explanations for why these things happen. But when there's real pain, it's hard to find a good answer. That's why we have to pull together and take care of one another. It's like my sister says in her newspaper ads: 'Everybody needs somebody to take care of them, and it's the taking care of that makes us sweet.' That's why what I'm going to ask Hattie is something very simple. And I hope it's sweet, too, in her eyes."

Uncle Waldo then patted the pockets of his suit coat with his hand, as if searching for something valuable he'd stored there.

"Waldo," said Mother, now with a nervous, almost desperate laugh. "I *really* wish you wouldn't—"

And that's when Uncle Waldo pulled from his jacket an architectural sketch. "Hattie," he said nobly, "I want to propose that you reconsider letting me build that breezeway between our houses."

TWENTY-FiVE

The Four Back, Three Unders Club

It TURNED OUT CLEM WAS WANTED in three states under three different names: Clovis Morris, Clive Moonross, and Clem Monroe. He was finally arrested in Thayer, Missouri, not far from the Arkansas border.

It turned out he used the same scam in every state: selling prepaid cremation plans to unsuspecting folks. He didn't have a cremating machine or a license to cremate. If anyone happened to die while he was still in town, Clem simply dumped the body somewhere and gave the family a bag of burnt toast he'd pulverized in a blender along with a chicken bone or two. (I *knew* those ashes smelled like burnt Parker House rolls!)

It turned out Clem had pulled the same stunt in St. Louis, Missouri, Davenport, Iowa, and Alton, Illinois. If Digginsville had any claim to fame in the FBI investigation, it was that we were the only ones promised a six-passenger horse-drawn carriage. In just nine days, Clem collected more than two thousand dollars from people eager to giddyup and give a buck for the Digginsville horse and carriage.

It turned out the tooth that fell out of the catfish's mouth did indeed belong to Gail Rowland from California. Her family was so upset, they nearly had another wreck on Highway 60 when they came to claim Miss Rowland's body.

And of course, Clem Monroe knew all about Doc Lake when he asked me about it that Sunday when I met him in Uncle Waldo's backyard. Turned out he'd dumped Miss Rowland's body in the lake the night before. That was when I first saw him from my bedroom window. He'd used Old Mary to haul Miss Rowland's body and later, poor old Mr. Aubrey Bryant.

It turned out Mr. Bryant's body was eventually cremated by a licensed cremator in St. Louis. Aunt Josie paid a small fortune to have his ashes scattered over Busch Stadium, home of Mr. Bryant's beloved Cardinals.

It turned out Mother liked the breezeway Uncle Waldo built almost as much as he liked building it. Once it was finished, I couldn't remember a time when our house wasn't connected to Uncle Waldo's house on one side and Mamaw's on the other—or a time when I didn't set the dinner table for four.

It turned out Uncle Waldo didn't mind doing dishes, especially when Mother let me help him. So we started eating off the everyday china during the week and Mother's fancy wedding china on Sundays. Sometimes we even used Mamaw's crystal goblets for iced tea.

It turned out it took only seconds for Uncle Waldo to oil the squeak out of our screen door. Mother admitted it had been bugging her for years. She even let him fix the toaster so it didn't burn every single piece of toast she made.

It turned out I used my ten tickets to the Rialto Theatre to take Mother, Mamaw, Uncle Waldo, Aunt Josie, and me to the movies—twice—in August before school started.

It turned out that once Aunt Josie got over

having her heart broken (it took about ten days), she couldn't read enough about Mr. Clem's problems with the law.

"I've taken a subscription to the *St. Louis Globe-Democrat*," she told me one day in late August when we were canning tomatoes at her house. "That's where his trial will be. You think we oughta go watch? Let's talk your mama into it, want to?"

"She won't go on account of her motion sickness," I said.

But it turned out she did go. We all did. Watching a jury convict Clem Monroe of seventy-four counts of fraud, conspiracy, obstruction of justice, money laundering, and tax evasion was the best entertainment any one of us had ever seen. By the end of the trial, Mr. Clem looked like the tired old snake handler who took tickets at the Traveling Reptile Museum.

It turned out the Traveling Reptile Museum was parked in front of Swisher's Grocery when we got back from St. Louis. Aunt Josie said the day contained an embarrassment of riches. I agreed.

It turned out twenty-two years after Clem's Crematorium came and went, Danielson Family Funeral

Home began offering cremation services for many of the same reasons Clem told Aunt Josie and me. Except, of course, for Uncle Seneca. There was no Uncle Seneca, dead or alive.

But there were at least seven women scattered across the United States who thought they were married or engaged to Mr. Clem. As far as I know, not one of them put up a fight for him, especially not Aunt Josie. After a while, she just laughed the whole thing off.

It made me wonder if the reason Aunt Josie laughed so much was because she cried so hard. Or maybe it was the reverse. Maybe life was like one big "Swap Line." In addition to trading things with other people, you swapped feelings with yourself during tough times.

After the crash, Mother swapped being sad for being mad. Uncle Waldo swapped feeling whatever a person's supposed to feel after a war for feeling shy. Aunt Josie sometimes swapped laughing for crying. Mamaw swapped feeling old and sad for acting young and silly. But maybe that was another kind of swap.

I didn't have any emotions there for a while. After the crash, I guess I swapped feeling something bad for feeling nothing at all—that is, until Mr. Clem came to town and scared me back to life.

But that's why you have to admit that in a strange way, Clem was good for us. He was somebody for Aunt Josie to love, for Mother to loathe, and for me to investigate. He gave Uncle Waldo someone to be compared to. He gave us all a reason to keep living that first summer A.D.

Clem brought us together in a way the crash hadn't, and for that I will always be grateful.

By the end of summer, I still divided my life into Before the Crash (B.C.) and After the Deaths (A.D.). But now I had a new, more entertaining way to divide my life: Before Clem and After Clem. And unlike the plane crash, which I could do nothing about, I could do something about Clem. And I did.

+   +   +

When school started again that fall, Mother let me spend a few afternoons a week at Aunt Josie's house while she worked at the beauty parlor.

"Daralynn, do you remember the nightmare I told you I had about getting locked in Clem's cremating machine?" Aunt Josie asked one September day as she rolled out pie crusts. "Well, I got burned all right, didn't I? That's why I never go to Hot Springs. I'd put my money on the wrong horse."

We both laughed.

"I'm just awful glad your mama was there for me when I was taking it so hard," she continued. "It did me a world of good when she came down and sat with me on my porch that night."

That's when it hit me: Mother had found someone to take care of. And it was Aunt Josie, of all people. And she had good hair, thanks to me.

"I think it helped her, too," I said. "That night, I mean."

"'Course it did," Aunt Josie said, plopping the limp dough into a pie pan and then crimping the edges.

As the pie crust browned, I couldn't help wondering what in the world Aunt Josie had done or said that made Mother break down like that. Mother, who never cried. Mother, who held everything in so tight after the crash. I was dying to know how it'd all happened.

"Emotions can take you by surprise," Aunt Josie said a half hour later when we were filling the warm crust with sugared apple slices. "Hold your emotions in too long and you turn into a volcano, all hot and mad, like you're just waiting to erupt. It's the same reason I poke air holes on the top crust. It's so the filling can breathe while it's cooking and not explode inside my stove."

She popped a sugared apple slice in her mouth and handed me one. It was deliciously crisp and sweet. Aunt Josie always seemed to know what I wanted even when I didn't.

While the pie baked, I helped Aunt Josie peel potatoes for dinner.

"Speaking of your mama," Aunt Josie said, "I've been meaning to ask you a question about her, but I don't want to hurt your feelings."

"Just ask me," I offered, cautiously.

"Well, you know I love my *Le Frenchie* haircut," she said. "But how would you feel if I started having your mother shampoo and style it for me? Would you mind?"

"Nah," I said. "I've pretty much given up my hair business."

The truth was, I wanted to spend more time writing than fixing hair, anyway. I was thinking about writing a whole book about Clem.

"You can always help me with cleaning and

cooking if you need some walking-around money," Aunt Josie said. "But I'd like to give Hattie another chance to do my hair, if she will."

"She will," I said.

And she did. Beginning that fall, and for as long as I could remember, Aunt Josie had a ten o'clock hair appointment with Mother every Saturday morning. I made a point to try to be at the beauty parlor then, too, just to hear those two talk.

"So I've got this new gentleman at my house," Aunt Josie began one Saturday morning. "His name's Mr. Harold P. Barnstubble. Would you believe he passes gas every morning at seven o'clock on the dot? Hattie, you think I'm exaggerating, but I'm not. He's like a regular rooster. I don't even have to set my alarm clock anymore. I can hear him all the way downstairs. *Toot toot toooooooot!* It's like a train rolling through the second floor of my house. Every morning at seven o'clock on the dot."

Mother laughed and laughed. The sound of those two women—the strongest women I would ever know in my entire life—talking and laughing was better than any music I ever heard.

After every hair appointment, Aunt Josie gave

Mother a big hug. The first time she did it, I could tell the gesture surprised Mother. She wasn't sure whether to hug back or not. She didn't. But at least she didn't flinch. And she didn't get mad.

Mother wasn't mad anymore. The world had changed—again.

And dare I admit the first thing I thought when I saw that hug? Bud Mosley's cracked aquarium. Maybe some things *could* be cracked without being broken. Maybe a heart could.

Pretty soon, Uncle Waldo started coming to the beauty shop on Saturday mornings, too. He brought glazed donuts and sat in the shampoo chair, talking and laughing with them. I realized that even though it'd been a rough year filled with death and betrayal and heartache, we were just about the four luckiest people on the planet.

That's when we formed a club: Mother, Aunt Josie, Uncle Waldo, and me. We called ourselves the Four Back, Three Unders. Over time, we became the We're Back—Until We're Under(ground) Club.

Uncle Waldo says we're going to make a banner and march in the Fourth of July parade one of these years. When we do, you can be sure that Mamaw will be right there with us, pushing her dolls in a baby carriage.

It turned out I finally just let Mamaw have all my dang dolls. Because everybody needs somebody to take care of them, even dolls.

TWENTY-SIX

Grounded for Life

In OCTOBER, JUST BEFORE the first anniversary of the crash, Mother asked if I wanted to go to the cemetery with her and make a flower bed around the family gravestone.

"I think we should plant a lilac bush and some roses," she said.

"You said you'd vomit if you ever smelled another rose," I reminded her.

"I'm getting past that," Mother replied.

I was, too. So we borrowed Old Mary from Aunt Josie, who also loaned us a rake, a shovel, and a pair of gardening gloves for Mother.

It was my idea to clear a spot to plant Big Boy tomatoes every summer in memory of Wayne Junior.

Mother liked that idea. But once we made a place for the roses, the lilac bush, and the tomato garden, there wasn't room left around the granite gravestone to plant anything for Daddy.

I told Mother that Daddy didn't like flowers much, anyway. "He liked casseroles tons better," I said. "I'll learn to cook some of his favorite dishes. We can remember him that way."

"Are you suggesting we branch out from our Schwan's diet?" Mother asked, smiling slyly. "Don't worry. I'm ready to resume cooking duties."

"I can help," I said. Because I really did want to learn how to cook. But I also wanted to think of a good way to remember my dad.

I thought twice before asking my next question, but I couldn't resist.

"Was I really his favorite?" I said, kneeling in the grass and smoothing the dirt in the future tomato bed.

"Your father and I didn't have favorites," Mother said. She had taken off the gardening gloves and was gathering up Aunt Josie's tools.

"But you *said* at your living funeral—" I started. Then I stopped. Maybe I'd misheard her. Maybe I was just wishing she'd delivered that postcard from Daddy.

"Lilac Rose was more like me, that's all," Mother said, almost like she was apologizing.

"So I *was* Daddy's favorite!" I concluded, smacking the dirt with my hands.

Mother set the tools down and came over to where I was sitting. She pulled me up so I was standing in front of her. Then she took my grimy hands in hers and stared me in the eye.

"If Daddy'd had a living funeral, do you know what he would've told you?" she asked.

"Nope," I said. "No idea."

Mother looked like she might start crying. But instead, she smiled and squeezed my hands hard. "That from the moment you were born, you were the apple of his eye."

"Really?"

"Really. Do you know what he wanted to name you?"

"What?"

"Waynette," she said, closing her eyes as if the word hurt her brain. "You are indebted to me for sparing you from that."

Waynette? Waynette?! We laughed for five minutes about that. Then I decided I needed to swap Mother something really good for that other thing she'd told me. I pretended to fiddle with the handle on Aunt Josie's rake.

"You were an awful good mother to Lilac Rose," I said. "That's what she would've told you if she'd had a living funeral. And you kept Wayne Junior from being a complete derelict."

She laughed. "I did my best."

The sun was warm that day. Crisp autumn leaves covered the ground. I couldn't resist kicking them around for a bit. I remembered that's what I'd been doing when Jimmy Chuck Walters came to our house to tell us the news about the plane. How it'd fallen from the sky. How they'd fallen, just like leaves from a tree, in the fall. And here it was again, fall.

"Do you miss them?" I asked Mother in a quiet voice.

"Every day," she said. "Every single day."

"Me too. I'm just afraid—" I stopped.

"What?" she asked. "What are you afraid of?"

And that's when I started crying. Big, fat messy tears rolled out of my eyes and down my face.

"Honey, what?" Mother said. "What are you afraid of?"

It was hard to talk because of how hard I was crying. I didn't know where all the tears were coming from. Once they started pouring out, I wasn't sure they'd ever stop. My emotions had snuck up on me, right there in the cemetery.

"What?" Mother asked.

I couldn't say it. It was too scary. As scary as Mr. Clem was, this was ten times scarier. Twenty times. A hundred times scarier.

"Tell me what you're afraid of," Mother said, wrapping her arms around me. "Tell me."

"That I'm going to forget them," I said.

She hugged me harder. "You never will. Never. I can promise you that. You can't forget them because they're all around you. Everywhere you look, everything you do, you'll feel them. You'll see them."

It came to me in a flash of inspiration while we were still at the cemetery. I asked Mother if I could return Old Mary to Aunt Josie's when we got home. There was something I needed to talk to her about: a way to remember Daddy.

When Aunt Josie heard what I wanted, she opened her metal address book and wrote down the name of a business in Kankakee, Illinois, along with a street address. I sent a letter to the company that very day.

Three weeks later I had what I wanted: five little

brass plaques with the words: WE ARE INDEBTED TO WAYNE T. OAKLAND, SR. FOR MAKING THIS POSSIBLE.

I glued one of the plaques on Daddy's tackle box. He would've liked that. Then I glued the second plaque on the wall of the breezeway to Mamaw's house. I attached the third one in the breezeway to Uncle Waldo's house. I used rubber cement to glue the fourth plaque to the dashboard of Old Mary.

And the fifth plaque? I keep it on my writing desk. Because I wouldn't have been possible if it hadn't been for Daddy. And odd as it might sound, writing every day with that little plaque on my desk keeps me grounded, just like all those dolls keep Mamaw grounded. Like tinkering with the breezeway keeps Uncle Waldo grounded. Like caring for her gentlemen keeps Aunt Josie grounded.

And like I keep Mother grounded.

All that time she thought she was the one who grounded me as a punishment. And she surely did in the B.C. era.

But in that first year A.D., I was the one who grounded Mother. And I intend to keep her grounded for the rest of her life.

ACKNOWLEDGMENTS

I would never have written this book if I hadn't wandered into Debi Gasperson Baird's hair salon in Mountain Grove, Missouri, almost twenty years ago. There I met a woman who can tell a better story while shampooing hair than I could ever hope to write. I wish I could attach a little brass plaque to the front cover of every copy of this book with the words: "I am indebted to Debi Gasperson Baird for all the stories she's told over the years about how she learned to style hair with her mother at their family funeral home after the death of her father and brother." Thank you, Debi, for letting me borrow your breezeway, your Salisbury steak TV dinners, and especially your aunt Peg, who became Aunt Josie. And I'm sorry I still haven't learned how to blow-dry my hair correctly.

I am also grateful to my nieces, Flora Klise and Eliza von Zerneck, as well as my nephews, Lorenzo and Sebastian von Zerneck. The character of Clem was born one winter night several years ago when the five of us were trying to make up a scary story together in the dark. Clem wasn't a cremator then, but he was certainly creepy. I don't think any of us slept very well that night.

Thanks to my wonderful editor, Liz Szabla, for always asking the right questions and for trusting me to find the story I'm trying to tell. Thanks to my first reader and brother, James Klise, for his wise suggestions written in pencil in the margins of my early drafts. And to my dear friends Joyce McMurtrey, Sherry Huffman, all my pals at Episcopal Church of the Transfiguration in Mountain Grove, Missouri, whose names I couldn't help borrowing for the denizens of Digginsville, and to Tim Bryant, who now trusts me to cut his hair: Thank you all for keeping me grounded.